LEE

Victory at Gettysburg

What if Lee had won the pivotal battle at Gettysburg?
An alternative history

The Battle of Gettysburg

Day One -- July 1, 1863 -- An Accidental Collision

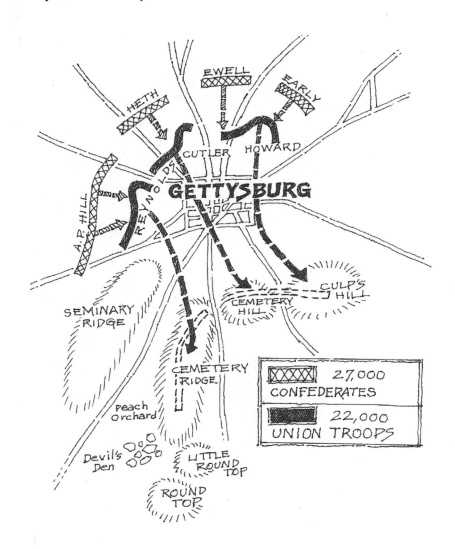

EWELL

HETH

EARLY

CUTLER

HOWARD

REYNOLDS

A.P. HILL

GETTYSBURG

CULP'S HILL

CEMETERY HILL

SEMINARY RIDGE

CEMETERY RIDGE

Peach Orchard

Devil's Den

LITTLE ROUND TOP

ROUND TOP

⨉⨉⨉⨉	27,000 CONFEDERATES
▓▓▓▓	22,000 UNION TROOPS

LEE

Victory at Gettysburg

❧❦☙

What if Lee had won the pivotal battle at Gettysburg?
An alternative history

Milton Norman Franson

2017

LEE
Victory at Gettysburg

An alternative history

For information, email: mfransonart@yahoo.com

or by USPS mail to: M.N. Franson, P.O. Box 2004
                        Liverpool, NY 13089

ISBN-13: 978-1975681333
ISBN-10: 1975681339
Library of Congress Control Number: 2017916404
CreateSpace Independent Platform, North Charleston, SC

Cover photo: Public Domain copy of Robert E. Lee portrait
(original 1863 photo by Julian Vannerson)

CreateSpace Independent Publishing Platform
North Charleston, South Carolina

Dedicated to

Roy & Jeff, fans of the Battle of Gettysburg

LEE

Victory at Gettysburg

CONTENTS

A New Nation

PART TWO An Inglorious Peace, An Elusive Dream

Battle Positions -- July 2, 1863

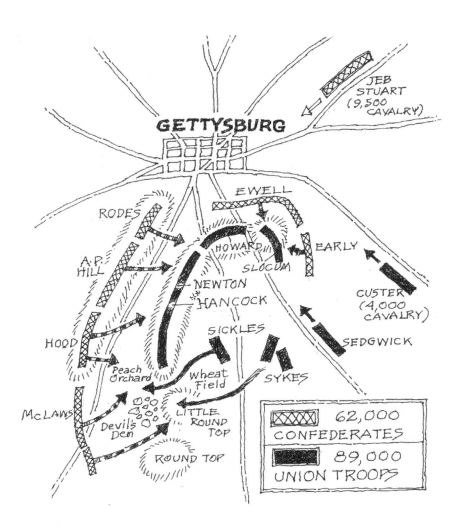

Prologue

Conventional wisdom says that Gen. Robert E. Lee lost the decisive battle at Gettysburg because of a bad decision to gamble everything on a risky frontal attack against a heavily fortified position. He sent Lt. Gen. Pickett's 12,500 infantrymen up an open, mile wide slope into the face of a well-entrenched enemy waiting atop a ridge bristling with cannon and rifles left, right and center. It was an apparently suicidal mission against a strong point in the enemy lines, appropriately named Cemetery Ridge. And it was unlike Lee's usual strategy. Normally he threw his entire force against the enemy in one simultaneous, well-coordinated two or three-pronged attack. But according to most reports of the battle, on the critical third day, only four-fifths of Lee's army were engaged during Picket's frontal attack. The fifth critical unit was missing. Where was Jeb Stuart's 9,500 man cavalry? And where was the coordinated support during Picket's charge up the hill? How could Lee have executed such a disjointed attack?

The problem with this assessment of Lee's battle plan is that this is not Lee. At such a critical point in his campaign against a numerically superior army, this is not the strategy of an acclaimed "military genius." No, a vital element of the Confederate battle plan seems to be missing on that third day at Gettysburg. There is something terribly wrong with the accounts of this battle. "Conventional wisdom" in this case seems to be in error.

According to one notable Southern cavalry officer who gained fame as a brilliant tactician, *what really happened on that fateful day was a failure by Lee's generals to follow through on his battle plan.* We can listen to Major John Mosby, "The Gray Ghost" who led guerrilla raids around, into and through the Union Army. Mosby said that what actually happened at Gettysburg was a totally unexpected case of misjudgment by Lt. General Longstreet, wrong timing by Lt.

General Ewell and most critical, the failure of Jeb Stuart to carry out his assigned attack on the rear of the Union lines.

And so, the great "what if" as nourished by generations of fans of the underdog, and nostalgic Southern schoolboys reliving the great battle is what would have happened if Lee's daring five-pronged battle plan had succeeded? What if the gray-clad army had split the Union line in two and destroyed each half piecemeal. What if the rebels had caused the wholesale surrender of the trapped boys in blue? If Union Gen. Meade surrendered his sword to Lee, what then? How might have Northern politicians reacted if Lee had defeated this Union Army of the Potomac, as he so ambitiously planned to do once they clashed?

John Mosby in his memoirs says Lee's main strategy in his invasion of the North was to move the battleground away from his exhausted Virginia. His plan was to let his army live off the fruits of the rich Pennsylvania farm country, all the while threatening Washington, D.C. and the Union cities of Baltimore and Philadelphia. Mosby states in his memoirs that Lee attempted to gather his forces at the pass below South Mountain near Cashtown, Pennsylvania, just a few miles west of Gettysburg. Gettysburg was *NOT* Lee's choice of a battleground, but once his vanguard became embroiled in a fight there with the Union vanguard, only then, according to Mosby, did Lee accept that battleground, on a point of honor.

To disengage the enemy, abandon the battlefield, then regroup his forces at South Mountain was a dishonorable choice for Lee. It was a military maneuver that a bold, proud warrior who held Napoleon as his ultimate war hero could never bring himself to do. In the prevailing code of war, it was not the honorable thing to do, and to General Robert E. Lee, honor came before duty, country or caution.

Caution was the strategy of Lee's old veteran war-horse, Lt. Gen. James "Old Pete" Longstreet. In preparing for the invasion of the North, Lee had agreed with Old Pete to forage his troops in Pennsylvania and so draw the Union Army of the Potomac away from the

South; but to be defensive rather than take the offensive. Longstreet cautioned that the Army of Northern Virginia numbered only 72,000 while he estimated the Army of the Potomac at possibly 100,000.

Old Pete was cautiously defensive, while Lee as a student of Napoleon, was an innovative and bold gambler on the battlefield. Lee often followed Napoleon's strategy of splitting his forces into three or four units, then maneuver them into advantageous positions surrounding his compacted enemy. Then in a surprise, coordinated series of maneuvers, he would bring them all together simultaneously against an enemy who was forced to defend itself from every direction. It was like hounds attacking a bear from all sides at once. But it required precise coordination; all units must work as one to succeed. And it was therefore risky. This was the battle plan that Mosby believed was Lee's strategy at Gettysburg.

Like Napoleon, Lee had forged a string of stunning victories against larger enemy forces, and like Napoleon, sooner or later one bold battle plan was doomed to unravel. For Napoleon it was Waterloo; for Lee, the audacious and highly risky strategy unravelled at Gettysburg.

But what if Lee had smashed the Union army at Gettysburg? Would that have driven Lincoln to accept a failed union as the price of a negotiated peace? Would Grant, Sherman and Sheridan have hastened back East from their victory at Vicksburg and beaten back a rejuvenated Army of Northern Virginia? Would Gen. Johnston have marched back home from Tennessee and joined Lee? And most important of all, would England's growing need for King Cotton to feed its textile mills force her to side with the Confederate States of America? Would England's voracious industrial revolution require her to ensure the importation of Southern cotton? Was a Southern victory in England's best interest? Economically, yes; politically, no.

If the states below the Mason-Dixon line became a sovereign nation, how would they have fared? That might have been the most intriguing twist in the South's battle for state's rights. A nation of 4.5 million European descendants gripping the chains of 3.5 million African slaves would have presented a dangerous situation for the plantation society. They were holding a lion by the tail. They would not dare let go, yet how long could they maintain their grip?

Southern statesmen had lived with their unique dilemma since before their war of independence, yet they could neither resolve the problem among themselves nor allow anyone else to dictate the terms of its resolution. It was the elephant in the room that Southern gentlemen of the time preferred to remain unmentionable, if not invisible.

Let's suppose that Lee had won a great victory at Gettysburg. What then? Would the dominoes have tumbled in favor of the Confederate States? Would they then be free to continue their life of selective privileged gentility? What should we suppose would have eventually happened? That is a scenario that no one's crystal ball can foresee. The outcome could take one generation or twenty to unfold. Parts of it have already played out since the actual Civil War's end, but the final act has yet to be performed.

The story that follows is pure fiction, and the real final chapter is waiting to be written.

M.N. Franson
July 2013
150th Anniversary of
the Battle of Gettysburg

PART ONE

THE
GLORIOUS
WAR

GETTYSBURG

Corporal Ralston's Cornfield Crawl
(Almost Midnight, July 1, 1863)

"God created War
so that Americans could learn geography"
Mark Twain

Beuford Forrest Ralston was a skinny 17 year old apprentice harness maker from Waynesboro on the Shenandoah when he went to the county courthouse and signed up to go fight the Yankees. He'd never heard of Gettysburg, let alone Pennsylvania. His world began and ended in the most beautiful river valley in the Great Dominion of Virginia. There was no other world, and in that world there was no other military God to look up to than General Robert E. Lee, the old man affectionately called "Marse Robert" by his devoted soldiers.

That Beuford had survived to his 18th birthday was no pure miracle. Firstly, he was so skinny as to be almost invisible when he ran sideways, left hand forward on his rifle, as his father had told him to do in battle. "Expose yerself little's possibly," he'd instructed Beuford. Corporal Ralston ran like his coon dogs, low to the ground, and hit the dirt soon's he heard the canisters whistling. His uniform had taken hornets of lead and bits of jagged shrapnel but so far, only one leg had gotten as much as a scratch. That was at Chancellorsville, where the dead lay stacked like autumn cordwood. "S'me lucky rabbit's foot," explained Private Ralston when Captain Sturtevant gave Beuford his Corporal's stripes.

Now, the Shenandoah Valley apprentice harness maker, who did-

1

n't know Pennsylvania from Vermont, was flat on his belly in a cornfield on a hot July night just outside the little Yankee town of Gettysburg. Beuford had been crawling around cornstalks many a dark night hunting midnight coons back home. Sure it was a long way up the wide slope to the top of Culp's Hill, where he and the boys had watched them dumb Yanks dig their asses wet in the hot July sun. Just so's they'd have some dirt in front of their artillery pieces so's his Shenandoah riflemen wouldn't get such a clean shot at them while them Yanks lobbed their hot shrapnel canisters at General Jubal T. Early's infantrymen, Corporal Ralston included.

The night was midnight blue and Beuford could see the Yankee watchfires glowing above the last 100 yards of the cornfield, where the stalks gave way to a 50 yard wide swath of hay. Some ingenious Pennsylvania German farmer had heard of Mr. Jefferson's idea of "contour planting" and layering your crops, or so the smart guys had told Beuford's pa. Anyway, two dozen Virginia coon hunters could easily crawl all the way up to rifle range and pick off any yank that cared to man one of those cannon up on the ridge. Beuford'd tell his Captain, who'd pass along the news to Marse Robert. But first he had to complete his mission. First he had to count the number of cannon, and as well's he could, how many soldiers were up there along this enemy line. For that last part he'd have to get awfully close and pray no one brought their dogs with 'em. Be a dang fool that'd bring a dog here, thought Beuford. But hell's bells, them's some dumb-assed Yanks up there. No tellin' what they dragged around with 'em. "Hookers" he'd heard.

Just in case a dog sniffed him, Beuford brought his coon magic with him. Tucked in a sack tied to his belt was a day old skunk skin. His nose'd got neutralized to it after the first half hour of crawling. But up here, with just the last 25 yards to the line of cannon mouths, he'd whip out that skunk skin in case a Yankee dog sniffed or heard

2

him. For sure the dog'd know enough to turn tail. Maybe even a Yankee nose would catch the scent.

Corporal Ralston finished tallying the last five Union cannon carriages. How many more were backed up in the woods behind, he couldn't know. Nor could he have any way of estimating how many Union soldiers were in the tents he could see from their campfires and flickering tent glows. That'd be up to the big boys to figure out; once he reported back to Captain Sturtevant.

He heard the rustling in the hay ahead, but not the hound's growl he feared. Beuford felt the hair on his neck stiffen. Then he recognized the red glow of a pair of coon eyes staring at him.

"You damn coon couldn't smell me coming?" fumed Beuford under his breath. Well take this, ya varmint, he thought as he reached for the skunk skin. The red eyes turned and he heard it scamper up toward the cannoned ridge when he flung the skin at it. Then he carefully turned to crawl back down into the cover of the cornfield.

"Jesus! It's a god-damned skunk! Throw a stick at the sucker before it gets up here!" Beuford heard the excited Yankees working up a lather over his little old coon routed in its nightly corn raid by a flung skunk skin. He chuckled to himself and slithered easily back to his lines.

Corporal Ralston sipped his tin cup of chicory "coffee" while he told Captain Sturtevant all he had seen and counted up there on the Union ridge. "They's mighty strong, Captain. Even's they's jest Yanks what couldn't hit the ass end of a mule with a broom standin' in a stall, Ah sure's hell'd never wanna try to drive em off that hill. Not lessen Ah had ten thousin V'ginians with me, Ah wouldn't." He drained his cup and wiped a sleeve across his mouth.

"Might take a few rifle boys up in the cornfield at night tho, an' pick off a few fools lollin' round the campfires."

"Well, yah, you might pick off a few Yanks like that, but that wouldn't be very sportin' now, would it Corporal? And it wouldn't remove all those artillery pieces now, would it? We'll see. We'll see what Jubal Early and General Ewell and the Old Man have to say about those entrenched fortifications."

Crossroads
June, 1863

Ten roads converged at Gettysburg. They radiated outward like the positions of hands on a clock. Due south out of Gettysburg ran the Tanneytown Road at six o'clock, with the Emmitsburg Road leading to the southwest at the 7:00 position. At roughly 8:00 was the Hagerstown Pike. At 10:00 was the Chambersburg Pike, at 11:00 ran the Mummasburg Road and at high noon the Carlisle Road ran due North. At 1:00 was the Harrisburg Road, 2:00 was the York Road, with Hanover Road at 3:30 running slightly to the south of East. Snaking through the town almost east to west was the Gettysburg & Hanover Railroad. Running off to the southeast at 4:30 was the Baltimore Pike. It was the busiest road, bringing a steady stream of the produce from the rich southern Pennsylvania farms to the hungry fish and crustacean-eaters of populous Baltimore. Though the citizens preferred their delicious crab cakes and steamed Chesapeake blue crabs, they complemented their diet with the field produce of Pennsylvania. Soon however, the southern flow of farm wagons would be interrupted by a steady stream of blue-clad horse soldiers hasting north towards Harrisburg.

It was the fact of its strategic location where so many roads con-

verged from all points of the compass that inevitably caused two op-
posing armies to unexpectedly bump into each other on the streets of
Gettysburg in late June, 1863.

Modern day generals appreciate the fact that armies must move
and maneuver as efficiently as possible. Vehicles move best on a dry
road. Even horses get bogged down in a muddy field, especially mid-
19th century horses and mules pulling heavy artillery pieces, as did
Union and Confederate forces in 1863. Henry V learned the signifi-
cance of horses in a muddy field at Agincourt, as did German generals during their Russian Campaign, as did Mssr. Bonaparte on his
parade route to Moscow and his slogging rout back to Paris.

June, 1863 was very hot in Maryland and southern Pennsylvania.
Two massive groups of men, mules and horses, each with long lines
of supply wagons, snaked their slow way north, across the Potomac
River. One headed towards the Pennsylvania capital at Harrisburg on
the Susquehanna River, the other cautiously following 40 some miles
to the east, flanking its foe with the intention of keeping its main
force always between the enemy army and Washington, D.C.

The massive group to the west was led by a fastidiously dressed
56 year old Virginia plantation and slave owner, whom his adoring
troops affectionately called "Marse Robert". He wore a wide-
brimmed gray hat over his white mane, just about the color of his
dappled gray steed, "Traveller." His uniform was a butternut gray,
trimmed with gold buttons and lapels with three gold stars. He rode
with an erect military bearing, an inspiration to his men as well as to
his subordinate generals. Ahead of him marched the first of his three
corps of 22,000 men each, newly reorganized from the two corps of
33,000 each that had beaten back Gen. Joseph Hooker's 113,000
men at the battles of Fredericksburg and Chancellorsville, where
General Robert E. Lee had lost his favorite general, his "right arm,"
"Stonewall" Jackson. The Stonewall had been shot off his horse by

"friendly" fire as he reconnoitered the field ahead of his troops. Now without his right arm, Lee sought to make his command more efficient by splitting Jackson's corps into two and putting new generals in charge of the three reorganized corps.

Lee's First Corps was commanded by Lt. Gen. James Longstreet. The new Second Corps was led by Lt. Gen. Richard Ewell. The new Third Corps went to the command of Lt. Gen. A.P. Hill. Absent from this strung-out infantry and artillery procession was the Cavalry Division of 9,500 horsemen under Maj. Gen. J.E.B. Stuart. Lee had given him the open-ended instructions to follow in the rear of the Union Army, now 30-50 miles to the east of Lee and harass and report Hooker's position as he followed Lee's march northward.

Lee's orders to Jeb Stuart, his "eyes and ears", were general: "after crossing the Potomac (whether by the eastern or western route) you must move on and feel the right flank of Ewell's troops (in Lee's vanguard, moving towards Harrisburg, Pennsylvania), collecting information about the enemy and gathering supplies when available."

From Stuart, Lee had received details of the Union's army strength, movements and intentions as passed on through a remarkable guerrilla Captain who had repeatedly penetrated and raided around, into and through General Joseph Hooker's plodding Union Army. Stewart's irregular, partisan guerrilla unit of 50-100 Confederate cavalrymen were led by a Captain John Stapleton Mosby, admiringly known as the "Gray Ghost" by the rebels and "that damned horse thief" by the men in blue.

Though he wanted a more wieldy army, Lee got something different than what he had at his Chancellorsville-Fredericksburg stunning victories. Where Stonewall Jackson always gave detailed and specific orders to his subordinates, which they had no option to alter or improvise upon, Lee's subordinates were accustomed to the opposite. Lee's orders were often vague, non-specific, something like:

"take that enemy position...if you think it practicable. Otherwise, use your best judgment as the opportunity presents itself." Therefore Gen. Lee's style was more fluid as the battle unfolded, while Jackson's corps was not accustomed to thinking for itself but to follow orders; to do or die.

The battle flag preceding Gen. Lee's 63,000 men strung out for 17 miles in a long line from the Potomac headed for Greencastle just over the Pennsylvania line, was an appropriately blood red field with a big star-studded "X" stamped across the bloody banner.

Forty some miles to Lee's east marched a long column of infantry, baggage trains, artillery, ammunition caissons; all smartly dressed in Union blue. Smarting from two recent defeats, they marched solemnly behind the same flag as had Washington, Jefferson, Henry "Light Horse" Lee, (Robert E. Lee's father), Francis "Swamp Fox" Marion and many other southern gentlemen-farmers and slave-holders. It was the same "stars and stripes"; same number of 13 stripes, but now with a few more stars.

The 94,000 men in blue wore generally similar uniforms and came from every Northern state, with the greatest numbers from the more populous Ohio, New York and Pennsylvania. Even the runty states of Maine and Rhode Island fielded proud units under their respective regimental colors. Unlike the solemn men in uniform blues, the Confederate regiments, although they were clad in a rag-tag conglomeration of grays, browns and whatever their mamas handed them, and often shoddily afoot, this determined band of brothers marched and sang like a victorious mob, which, after their successes at Chancellorsville and Fredericksburg a scant month earlier, they were. They felt invincible and were ready to follow "Marse Robert" into the jaws of Hell, or Pennsylvania, whichever came first.

Early Morning Thunder
5 am, July 1, 1863

"Unleash the Dogs of War!"   Wm. Shakespeare

On June 30th General Lee's three corps were strung out in a long column just over the Pennsylvania border. In the vanguard was a brigade of North Carolinians under Brig. Gen. Johnston Pettigrew. They had swung east of the main column to raid nearby Gettysburg and requisition supplies, paid for with worthless Confederate dollars. However, when they reached the western edge of town, they saw Union cavalry and infantry coming in from the east on the Baltimore Pike, so following Gen. Lee's orders not to engage the enemy until all the Confederate army had gathered at the foot of South Mountain some eight miles northwest of Gettysburg, they raced back to report to their corps commander, Lt. Gen. A.P. Hill, whose troops were closest to Gettysburg.

Hill did not believe any significant Union forces could have arrived in Gettysburg ahead of him, so he assumed they were perhaps just a small local militia unit. Yet he cautiously decided to send a strong force there to assess the situation, mindful that Lee had advised his corps commanders to initiate no significant action before the full Confederate force was gathered at Cashtown, under the shadow of South Mountain.

At dawn the next day, July 1st, Gen. Hill sent two brigades under Brig. Gens. James Archer and Joseph Davis into Gettysburg. Waiting for them on three ridges west of the village was a small cavalry division of the Union vanguard led by Brig. Gen. John Buford plus a small detachment of Union infantry.

Brig. Gens. Archer and Davis led their two brigades against the smaller force Buford had deployed to delay the Confederates until the vanguard of Union I Corps under Maj. Gen. John Reynolds arrived. By mid-morning the Confederate brigades had pushed the Union defenders out of their initial positions in the surrounding hills, and driven them onto even stronger defensive terrain in an arch of ridges north and west of town.

Late in the morning, Union Maj. Gen. Reynolds appeared with units of his I Corps and a fierce battle was joined. In response, Gen. Hill called up an entire division plus more brigades of Col. John Brockenbrough and Gen. Pettigrew into the seesaw fray. The Union forces were greatly outnumbered, and early in the fighting, Gen. Reynolds was killed and replaced by New York Maj. Gen. Abner Doubleday. However, Doubleday didn't field enough men either and the Union I Corps was being shredded by Hill's divisions.

In mid-afternoon, as the seesaw battle raged around Gettysburg, Lee's Second Corps divisions of Jubal A. Early and Maj. Gen. Robert Rodes arrived and slammed into Union positions around Oak Hill and Blocher's Knoll guarding the northern and western roads into town. The Union divisions reeled under the shock and retreated to the higher ground south of town at Cemetery Hill and Culp's Hill, where they regrouped and began to dig in.

Apprised of the unexpected situation, Lee, who had been in Cashtown waiting for his full army to assemble, then recalled Gen. Richard Ewell from foraging near Carlisle. Ewell and his troops could hear the thunder of battle as they quick marched south down the Carlisle Road towards the little town of Gettysburg. Quickly conferring with Lee, Ewell was told that Union forces had retreated to strategic high ground on Culp's and Cemetery Hill. Sensing the importance of those strong defensive heights, Lee ordered Ewell to "take Cemetery Hill...if practicable." By that loose command, Lee meant that Ewell must use his own battlefield judgment and gain the advantageous position if he could grasp and hold it, but not to pay too high a price if he judged it would take more men to fulfill the order.

Arriving on the battle scene playing out around Cemetery Hill, Ewell was unsure of the enemy strength on the heights, so he decided to send three companies in a feint up the slope and simultaneously attack both flanks with the remainder of his troops.

Leading the attack up the eastern side of Cemetery Hill were units of the 40th Virginia Infantry, "The Waynesboro Volunteers."

"Hey! Wally! That's us." yelled Private Beuford Forrest Ralston to his best friend, Wally Zebediah Brewster. Captain Sturtevant had just alerted his company to load their muzzleloaders and prepare to follow the Company Banner up the hill to drive the enemy off the ridge.

"Jee-suus! Beuford, this'll be my first action 'gainst them damn Yankees!! They'll sure as Hell wish they'd never tangled with the Waynesboro Volunteers!"

"Jus' keep yore dang'd head down Wally, an' run low to the groun' like I show'd yah."

Three hundred howling rebels screamed out their blood curdling Rebel Yell as they ran to the base of Cemetery Hill and pushed into thin bushes on the lower slope, all following their proud company banner dead ahead of Beuford and Wally.

Their Rebel howls were answered with a withering whistling of lead balls flying at them from the smoking barrels of 200 Yankee riflemen, all armed with the latest Sharps repeating rifles. Their firepower equalled 2000 rebel muzzleloaders. Nevertheless, the charging Waynesboro Volunteers responded with their own volley. Men fell and screamed and moaned as lead balls and bullets reaped their deathly harvest. But the odds of an enemy shell or shot hitting a running Beuford Ralston were about as slim as his side-ways silhouette. Through the confusion of gunfire and smoke, Private Beuford saw the banner bearer stumble and fall. The colors touched the ground in defeat.

"Goddammit, Wally! Grab the colors!" screamed Beuford. Before he knew what he was doing, Private Beuford Forrest Ralston grabbed the pole and flourished the company colors high over his head.

"Follow me, boys! C'mon you Volunteers! Go get them bastards!" A bullet hit the pole and nearly tore it from Beuford's grasp. Another knocked his hat off his head while a third tore through his shirt. Still Beuford ran ahead in the swirling gun smoke leading his hard charging and greatly diminished company. Then a strong hand spun him around and flung him to the ground. He stared dazedly into the contorted face of Captain Sturtevant.

"You crazy, boy? Di'nt you hear the bugle sound retreat? This is suicide! Gotta git back to our lines!" They raced back downhill as low to the ground as they could while Union bullets chased them like a pack of mad hornets. How they both made it back to their lines was a story the Waynesboro Volunteers told and retold for many a night thereafter.

"What's your name, Private?" said a sullen Captain Sturtevant.

"Beuford." He gripped the color's shaft with a hand still trembling from his adrenaline overload.

"No, Goddammit, Private! Your full name!" Beuford pulled himself up as straight and tall as he could.

"Private Beuford Forrest Ralston, 40th Virginny, Waynesboro Volunteeeers! Suuuh!" And he saluted crisply.

"You ain't no *Private*, no more, Beuford. You're *Corporal* Ralston now, and I'm damn proud of you! You're either the dummist jackass in Waynesboro, or you're the bravest man in my company.

Either way, you're promoted."

"Yesss! Suuurrh! Thank ya, Surrh" grinned Corporal Beuford Forrest Ralston.

Companies A and B had lost over a third of their men attacking the flanks of Cemetery Hill, while Beuford and Wally had been among only twenty surviving men of the eighty-nine who charged up the face of the hill. Assessing his losses and the strength of the Union defenses, General Ewell called off the feint and the attack. Sizing up the strong defensive position of the Union infantry and the arrival of more Union II Corps troops under Maj. Gen. Winfield Hancock, Ewell decided it was not "practicable" with the troops currently at his disposal. Cemetery Hill was now a fortress that any sensible commander understood could be easily defended in the classic 4-1 ratio. Ewell knew one Union defender could turn back every four Confederate attackers. He did not like those odds, so he deferred to Gen. Lee for further instructions or more troops. While Ewell's offensive stalled, Gen. Hancock furiously fortified his hilltop and awaited the arrival of the remaining Union infantry corps.

Somewhere to the northeast was Jeb Stuart's cavalry division, past York and headed for Carlisle, Pennsylvania. Stuart was expecting to join up with Gen. Ewell to reconnoiter the Union defenses of Harrisburg, then swing south with his cavalry and a train of captured Union supply wagons and report back to Lee at Cashtown, Pa. near the South Mountain Pass rendezvous point. Unknown to Stuart, Gens. Hill and Early had already inadvertently engaged the vanguard of the Union forces led now by a cautious and wary Gen. George Meade, who only four days earlier had replaced Gen. Hooker as commander of the Army of the Potomac. This Union army had had its nose bloodied recently, not once but twice by the genius of Robert E. Lee, first at Fredericksburg and again at Chancellorsville.

General Robert E. Lee's master campaign for the Summer of 1863 had been to take his Army of Northern Virginia, now numbering almost 72,000 infantry, artillery and cavalry and bring the war into Northern territory, with the aim of influencing war-weary Northern politicians to clamor for a peace treaty. Lee also calculated that a Northern campaign would demonstrate to a fence-sitting England that the time was ripe to recognize the Confederate States of America as a separate and independent country. England was hungry for Confederate cotton to feed its voracious textile mills. It feared the consequence of this source being choked off by a victorious Union and its vengeful politicians. No matter to England that it had abolished the slave trade while its cotton source lived off slavery and was determined to maintain its status quo.

Lee's secondary objective was to give relief to his war-ravaged Northern Virginia by drawing the Union Army of the Potomac out of Virginia and force it to defend the northern lifelines into Washington, D.C. His troops would live off the rich Pennsylvania farmlands while they harried cities, especially the capital, Harrisburg.

Fifty years earlier, another military genius had proclaimed that "an army marches on its stomach". Presumably the Corsican genius understood that supply lines and logistics were as important to the success of an army as was the troops' morale and leadership. Getting only three out of four right could sometimes prove fatal, even for a military genius.

The moment he heard that Lee had left Chancellorsville and was moving rapidly north, Abraham Lincoln gave orders for "Fighting" Joe Hooker to lead the Union Armies in hot pursuit. Just three days before his army reached Pennsylvania, "Fighting" Joe, in a dispute with his superiors over battle strategy, offered to resign. Lincoln eagerly accepted, and an indecisive Major Gen. Joseph Hooker was immediately replaced by a cautious Major Gen. George G. Meade and his second-in-command, arguably the best officer in the Union Army, Maj. Gen. John F. Reynolds.

Now in charge of the 94,000 man Army of the Potomac, a wary George Meade listened to two excited couriers in his tent on the evening of June 29th. The first to arrive was a Pennsylvania militiaman from Harrisburg. "We spotted a huge contingent of Confederate cavalry entering Carlisle this morning. We estimate about 15-20,000. It could be Jeb Stuart. They're camped around Carlisle and raiding the farms for supplies. And paying for their theft with Confederate Jeff Davis dollars."

Gen. Meade turned to his cavalry commander, Maj. Alfred Pleasonton, whose horse-soldiers had protected Meade's right flank ever since a chance meeting with Jeb Stuart three weeks earlier. "Alf, could that be Mr. Stuart, all the way up to Harrisburg?"

"It well could be. If so, he's got some mighty foot-sore horses to push 'em so far so fast. But one thing he doesn't have is no 20,000 men. When we last saw him we estimated only 5-7,000."

The second courier reporting to Gen. Meade was a cavalry sergeant attached to Brig. Gen. John Buford's Union cavalry division. "Gen. Buford sends this letter, sir."

Buford's note read as follows:

"Have engaged a Confederate advance force entering the town of Gettysburg. Against superior numbers we have taken up defensive positions on the hills to the northwest of town, but may not be able to defend. Will retrench on higher ground to the south of town, if necessary. Request urgent reinforcement before main Confederate force arrives."

Signed: Gen. John Buford

The Invincibles
June 9th- July 1, 1863

The Union Army was in no hurry to renew General Lee's acquaintance anytime soon. One factor in explaining Hookers' plodding shadow tactics and Meade's subsequent extra caution while pursuing Lee's march into Pennsylvania, was the constant nipping at the heels of the Union Army by Lee's dogged cavalry division of 9,500 troopers led by the dashing James Ewell Brown Stuart, affectionately known as Jeb to his men. Lee had given Stuart the vague order to flank the Union Army on the move while capturing supply wagons as the opportunity presented. This Stuart did, from early June through July 2nd. Unfortunately for Lee, Stuart was dogging Meade on his eastern flank, while Lee's army moved ahead on the west; many miles and 94,000 Union troops separating Lee from Stuart, his campaign's eyes and ears.

Twice in prior campaigns, Jeb Stuart had plagued the Union army. Once he had ridden his cavalry completely around the plodding Union force. Perhaps, as his mobile cavalry dogged Hooker's strung-out army, Stuart fancied he could do it again, and demoralize the Yankee troops as he had done in the past. Stuart's cavalry division was both feared and admired; feared by the Union as an invincible foe while lionized by Confederates as the epitome of Southern horsemen. But on the road into Brandy Station outside of Culpeper, Virginia on June 9th, early into the movement north, Stuart was caught sleeping in at dawn by an attacking Union cavalry division under Major General Alfred Pleasonton. Stuart repulsed the unexpected attack and though the Invincibles eventually drove Pleasonton back across the Potomac, Jeb Stuart's proud troopers now rode more cautiously along the Union flank, not quite so invincible as before.

Jeb Stuart then led his calvary brigades north through Maryland, dogging the Union army with Gen. Hoooker always keeping between the advancing Lee while protecting the approaches to Washington and Baltimore. By the time the first units of the Grand Army of the Potomac reached the eastern edge of Gettysburg, led by Brig. Gen. John Buford's cavalry division, Jeb Stuart had raced all the way north to Carlisle, Pennsylvania, just west of Harrisburg. Consequently, when the unexpected clash occurred on July 1st in Gettysburg, Stuart's cavalry was too far away to play a role. He arrived late in the day of the first clash and immediately reported to Lee.

The Architect of Gettysburg
July 1-7, 1863

Gettysburg was not the battlefield Lee would have chosen. His orders to his army as it moved strung out over the Pennsylvania border was to gather at South Mountain outside Cashtown, Pennsylvania. That terrain favored Lee. But now, unexpectedly, two of his generals had engaged the enemy at Gettysburg and inadvertently pushed the Union army into a favorable defensive position on high ground. Militarily, the Union army now held a fortress, which would force the attacking Lee to chose between a siege or an encircling multi-pronged attack. Robert E. Lee was a proud man, and a student of the great Napoleon. A siege was not in his nature and it was not a tactic suited to Lee's temperament. However disadvantageous it seemed for a smaller surrounding force to attack a larger force entrenched on high ground, Lee's proud, impetuous nature impelled him to initiate the boldest, most glorious strategy, as Napoleon would have done.

The other factor driving Lee to accept his role as fortress-attacker was his unshakeable belief that whatever happened on the battlefield, as in life, was in the hands of the Almighty. Men would fight the battles, but the outcome was determined by Providence. Lee was merely the instrument in the hands of God. Therefore, he never gave credit to himself for either victory or defeat. He quietly and humbly accepted whatever the fates decreed. It was not his fault if his impetuous strategy caused 10,000 men to become cannon-fodder. Just as it was not his glory to be proclaimed if those 10,000 men stormed an enemy position against overwhelming odds and swept the field to victory.

At Gettysburg, neither Lee nor Meade was the architect of defeat or victory. All this was up to a mightier force than Gen. Robert E. Lee or any other mere mortal. Or was it?

A Gathering of Generals
Seminary Ridge   Evening, July 1, 1863

"Marse" Robert sat his horse with his usual erect, military bearing, in spite of the pain. Traveller chewed the bit and shook his head, sensing something different in his master's rein. The General brought the binoculars up smartly and scanned the far knoll, known locally as Cemetery Hill.

"We'll need that little hilltop," he said matter-of-factly to no one in particular. Generals Ewell and Hill nodded in agreement as did the General's other lieutenants. Notably missing was General Lee's "right arm", the man who'd earned the name Stonewall. Jackson. He had taken friendly fire in the blindness of battle at Chancellorsville just three months earlier. He lay quietly under six feet of Northern Virginia soil.

"Send out scouts tonight to spy out the Union lines. I want to know Meade's strong points and where he's weakest. Tomorrow we'll probe his soft spots. And we must take that hill--Cemetery Hill."

As Lee and his generals watched from their vantage point on Seminary Ridge, a mile away the Grand Army of the Potomac was furiously entrenching into their defensive positions for their next encounter with the respected military genius leading the encircling Confederate army. Neither Lee nor Meade fully understood the numerical strengths of their adversary. Meade was determined to stop Lee's invading army as it continued a circular route that seemed poised to cut off Washington, D.C. from it's northern supply roads. Now Lee and Meade were faced off in a seemingly insignificant little farming town just over the Pennsylvania border.

General Lee had to put an uneasy trust in information assembled from various sources not yet proven reliable. His unease at the new pain that had travelled up his left arm and recently throbbed under his jaw, now broke out in a sweat across his shadowed brow. He need not worry that his perspiration on this hot July evening would alarm his lieutenants; they too sweltered in their gray woolen uniforms and gained little relief from the shade offered by their broad brimmed campaign hats. Ironic, too that woolen "union suits" added to their discomfort. No less was the discomfort of their adversarial brethren toiling in their dark blue woolens as they furiously entrenched themselves across the hay and wheat fields and up on the little hills and ridges.

Lee lay the field glasses down to the pommel and looked at each of his generals, quietly seated on their fidgety horses. They respectfully awaited some new hint from the old man that would foretell their and their waiting legions' fates. He had never let them down, in fact had amazed them with his coolness in commanding their stunning series of recent battlefield victories over often overwhelming numbers. He had his soldiers' undying devotion, and to a man the southern farm-boys revered the general they lovingly called "Marse Robert".

Only two of his subordinates withheld their full confidence in the Commanding General. They had been on the receiving end of his rashness twice when he got his "battle blood" up and quietly wondered if too much adrenaline in the heat of battle had altered his usually cool, detached judgment. Not even his surgeon suspected the true cause of The General's change of mood. But as he lowered the glasses with his right hand, Lee knew he could not then have performed the simple maneuver with his aching left arm. The same ache he'd felt now for two days throbbed all up the inside of his left arm, but now a new pain throbbed under his jaw. The nausea and faint dizziness came back as he quietly sat Traveller. He wiped his wet forehead as Gen. Hood observed the damp pale sweep over The General's face. "Sir, are you all right?"

"Just the heat, Mr. Hood. I'm too hot." He gazed into each man's face as a hint of a smile turned up the corners of his mouth. "Tonight we'll meet at sup and draw up the alternate plans." The General was in fit form again. He had good reason. All that first day of battle, his generals had swept Union forces from their initial defensive positions along the western edge of the town of Gettysburg with heavy Federal losses. From Herr Ridge, McPherson Ridge and Seminary Ridge, Lee's Generals Ewell and Hill had pushed the Union defenders south to a fishhook-shaped line extending from Culp's Hill and

Cemetery Hill in the north, and south along Cemetery Ridge towards two hills named Round Top and Little Round Top.

Yet, however much Lee's troops had outfought their adversary that day, General Ewell had inadvertently given the Union Army a strategic advantage late on the first day of conflict by failing to take Cemetery Hill from the beleaguered Union's I Corps. Late in the morning, I Corps's brilliant commander, Maj. Gen. John Reynolds was killed along with many of his troops. Meade replaced him with his most trusted subordinate, Maj. Gen. Winfield Hancock. Hancock proceeded to vigorously dig in, anticipating Lee's next day attack.

Lee's vague order to Ewell had been to take Cemetery Hill "if practicable." Though Ewell had the Union troops on the run, he had decided it was not "practicable" with the troops at his disposal, so he allowed the retreating I Corps to dig in on the critical defensive position on top of Cemetery Hill. He had awaited more specific orders and more aid from Lee. It never came.

The Confederate offensive had taken all day and now Lee and his generals looked out from atop Seminary Ridge and assessed the left flank defensive positions of the gathering Union Army. It was clear to all that Meade's troops had gained one of the strongest defensive positions that an army could ever hope for. But the nagging thought in Robert E. Lee's mind was not how to take Cemetery and Culp's Hill, it was rather will this feeling of nausea pass and will I be able to hold my saddle tomorrow when the critical time comes?

The Plan
Late at night, July 1st

The flickering oil lamps cast a Rembrandt-like glow over the bent figures of Generals Lee, Hill, Hood, Ewell, Johnson, Rodes, Early, McLaws, Anderson and Gordon. Missing were Generals James Longstreet, and George Pickett, still on the march from Chambersburg, Pa., thirty miles to the west, and Jeb Stuart, on his way from Carlisle and due anytime.

Lee and his generals had been two hours after sundown drawing the supposed field positions of the Union forces. Knowing their knowledge was incomplete, they had drawn up several alternative options, depending on which bit of information they agreed was most accurate. As always, Lee was the bold, imaginative field marshall, ever ready to exploit the enemy's weaknesses, real or perceived; ready to improvise as the battles ebbed and flowed. As always, his more conservative generals, all younger than The Old Man, cautioned a more careful maneuver. Thrust and parry, feint and retreat, advance when superior, flank where opportunity presented. Maintain order above all. None of these options came naturally to the impetuous field commander who now thrust a finger forcefully into the pivot point on the map spread before them.

"This is the fulcrum!" snarled the Old Man, with his finger on Cemetery Hill. "We must feint a major thrust over here at Culp's Hill, but it is *this* superior height we must secure at all costs. Then Meade's artillery becomes useless. His cannon will shoot over our heads and directly into the village." He quickly calmed himself down as he grasped his left arm solidly with his right hand. The move was

21

not lost on Gen. John Hood, who had noticed the same odd gesture three times in the past week.

"Let the Yankee farm boys dig themselves in from here to here and they have neutralized their maneuverability. Then we can dance around their flanks, hit them in the rear with the cavalry and let them sweat in the sun whilst we pick our points of attack at the time of our own choosing. I fear the plodding Lincoln Generals have set themselves up as dead meat in the center of their own bear trap. We'll have 'em, boys, in our own good time. In our own good time." He pulled the eyeglasses off his patrician planter's nose and folded them solemnly. He laid them down over an insignificant spot on the map labeled "wheat field", next to a "peach orchard".

All that day had been as hot as the previous. As evening fell and guns fell silent, Lee had sent his reserve cavalry units to work all around the Union Lines, trying to guess the actual enemy size and positions. But the terrain was hilly, often thickly wooded or views otherwise obscured, and the more information Lee and his staff collected, the more confusing the battlefield maps became. That night as Lee and his staff pored over the maps and the conflicting data, they grew increasingly frustrated. The Beast was gigantic, it had many tentacles, and most of them were hidden from view. And yet, a bold plan was forming in Lee's mind.

Gen. John Hood quietly observed the reddening of The General's neck, the pulsing of his neck artery and the mist of perspiration that he mopped periodically from his white forehead. Something was wrong. He had no medical experience, but he had seen his own father sicken and die suddenly from a stroke. He determined to say nothing to the others, certainly not to The Old Man, but he would ask the company surgeon in the morning. Meanwhile, The Old Man gave his marching orders for pre-dawn assaults on July 2nd by Gen. Jubal

Early and Maj. Gen. Edward "Allegheny" Johnson against the key positions: Culp's and Cemetery Hill, while elements of Longstreet's First Corps rolled up the Union left flank along Emmitsburg Road near the Round Tops.

"Take the High Ground!"
First Light, July 2, 1863

"Get there the furstess, with the mostess"
Nathan Bedford Forrest,
Confederate Lt. General

Corporal Ralston was roused from a fidgety sleep by his buddy Wally Zebediah Brewster's toe. "Sumpin's up, Beuford," whispered Wally. "I guess we're movin' out soon. I heard Capt'n Sturtevant talking marchin' orders with Howard. Sumpin's up, I reckin."

Their battalion, part of the 40th Virginia Infantry Regiment, "The Waynesboro Guards", was under the command of Major Lynville Perkins. The 40th was attached to Maj. General Jubal A. Early, who had marched his infantrymen into the town of Gettysburg with the vanguard of the Second Corps of Gen. Richard Ewell. Now on the morning of the second day's fighting, "Take the high ground of Culp's Hill and Cemetery Hill" was the order given to Maj. Gen. Ed Johnson and Gen. Early and their regiments that included Major Lynville Perkins' and Corporal Ralston's unit.

At 5 A.M. in the breaking dawn, Corporal Beuford Forrest Ralston and Wally Zebediah Brewster grabbed their packs and rifles and joined the assembling 40th Virginia Guards. Before they knew where they were headed they were fast-marching toward a hill named Culp's where it rose out of the morning mist, just south of the town. Already Brig. Gen. George Greene's New York defenders were lobbing canisters and cannon shells at the attacking Confederates, soon to be followed by a withering rifle fire from behind their strong defensive works on the crest of the hill.

Beuford Ralston ran sideways alongside his buddy Wally Brewster. "Je-suus, Wally, we're gonna drive them damned Yankees clear off that hill and into Kingdom Come!" Corporal Ralston heard the whistles singing towards them but before he could react, a tremendous roar deafened his eardrums at the same time as a flying Wally slammed into his right side. Beuford felt something like a rock crash into his right temple. Then all went black as he stumbled into the ground.

Watching the rapidly advancing lines of Confederate infantrymen was Private Alfred Werner Swanson of the 154th New York Infantry Regiment, commanded by Brig. Gen. George Greene. Private Swanson was a big, strong kid, an 18 year old lumberjack when he enlisted with the New York regiment from Jamestown, a little village nestled in the gentle Allegheny foothills of Chautauqua County in the far western end of New York State. "Hey you, Private Swanson!" Major Henry Loomis had admonished him the previous day. "Let me see that dirt fly!" Gen. Greene had pushed his weary brigade to dig a strong defensive breastwork along their section of the Union line spread atop the crest of Culp's Hill. Gen. Meade had advised his subordinates that the most likely point of attack by Lee would be against the flanks and center of the Union lines defending Cemetery Ridge and Culp's and Cemetery Hills. Now, Private Swanson and his fellow New Yorkers quietly awaited the onslaught of the gray clad infantrymen running towards them. "Hold your fire till I give the signal," Swanson's captain ordered his troops. "Let our cannon do their work first. Then take careful aim at the nearest rebel."

The heavy object that slammed into Corporal Ralston's right temple was Wally's head, now detached from his neck. When Beuford awoke, his head was buzzing and he felt as woozy as if his mule had kicked him in the head. He saw a bright blue sky above him and was conscious of the steady thunder of cannon and the staccato of massed gunfire somewhere up the hill. But why was he flat on his back, alone in the dewey grass? He shook the fog from his head and looked around. Next to him was a sprawled Wally, right leg strangely angled at the blue sky. Several of his fellow infantrymen also sprawled in twisted forms all around with many more lying still or crawling and moaning up on the slope where they'd been knocked down. Beuford saw the mess of dark blood soaking his neck and shirt, but oddly he felt no pain of wound. He then remembered the crash that knocked him down and knew he must have taken a hit. He moved his arms and legs and felt his head and neck. Everything worked fine except for the ache at his temple. Then he looked to his left in the grass and saw Wally's head, eyes wide open, for all the world admiring the beautiful blue sky of a warm July morning just south of the town of Gettysburg near the gentle slope of Culp's Hill.

"Did the boys took the hill?" wondered Corporal Ralston. They had not.

Incapacitated
Morning, July 2, 1863

Awake at dawn, Gen. Hood was told the surgeon was attending General Lee. Gastric attack they had explained. Hood was now alarmed. What if The General was incapacitated at the height of the upcoming battle? What if they had to delay The Plan? Who could execute the alternative plans if The Old Man was too sick to take to his horse? Lee's battles always depended on instant decisions depending on the flow of battle as it unfolded. That was his genius and his alone. No one else could improvise as The General could in the confusion of a raging, ever-changing battlefield.

General Hood went immediately to Lee's tent. What he saw shook him in his boots. General Lee's face was as white as his hair. Two doctors attended him. They looked up at General Hood and shook their heads. Quietly the surgeon general told him the news. "He's had a mild heart attack. We think he's stabilized, but any battle commanding in the next few days is out of the question. It'd probably kill him. He's resting now. We gave him laudanum powder to stabilize him. You can talk to him when he's awake. Maybe this time tomorrow. We'll see how he responds."

Lee's orders for the battle plan as he drew it up the previous night called for an early dawn attack on Culp's Hill and Cemetery Hill by Maj. Gen. Jubal Early and Maj. Gen. Edward "Allegheny" Johnson's Second Corps divisions. It was to be a feint, a "demonstration" maneuver, one of Gen. Lee's trademark improvising moves, that, depending on the Union response, was to turn into a full-scale attack if the situation developed favorably to Gen. Early.

Jubal Early was not only early this morning, he had jumped the gun ahead of Hood's and Hill's planned simultaneous attacks on the Union's southernmost positions. He did not know that upon seeing Lee's condition, Hood and Hill jointly decided to delay the attack plan until Gen. Longstreet arrived to take full command. And so, Gen. Early sent his troops on a sunrise "demonstration" assault against fortified Union forces atop Cemetery and Culp's Hills, not knowing he had no support and very slim odds of "taking the high ground."

Thinking and Waiting
Afternoon, July 2, 1863

"The supreme art of war is to subdue the enemy
without fighting"
Sun Tzu, The Art of War

General James Longstreet arrived late in the morning of July 2nd. His subordinate, Gen. George Pickett and the balance of his II Corps would arrive later that afternoon. Longstreet was surprised to see both armies dug in with only light peripheral skirmishes going on. But when he heard about Lee, he immediately understood the gravity of the situation. He was now commander. The responsibility was his. He convened a quick conference with the other generals.

"Where's Stuart?" asked Longstreet. No one knew. Only that Lee had met with him last night and had privately given Stuart instructions to take up a position to the extreme left flank of Ewell's position. What more, Stuart had not said and Longstreet assumed it was another of Lee's vague and flexible marching orders. Longstreet was perplexed. He would go to Lee the next day for a clarification of the battle plan; one that was already off on a wrong Early foot.

"What do we know of the Union positions, then?" Generals Hill and Heth apprised him of the previous day's events on the ridges to the north of town. They explained how they'd met an advancing unit of Union cavalry and an infantry detachment that they had driven onto some small hills to the northwest of the village. There they had attacked and driven the enemy south through town, with Generals Ewell and Early in pursuit. Gen. Heth's two brigades joined in along with Brig. Gens. Archer and Davis, moving south along the Chambersburg Pike. The initial skirmishes had developed into a fierce see-saw battle as each army added new infantry corps to the fray. At the end of the day, Lee's army had driven Meade's defenders south of the town and onto what now appeared to be very strong defensive positions. There had been severe losses on both sides, but Gen. Lee's men had fought well and had the Union army surrounded on their hills. How many were there, no one could guess.

"That's all we know, right now," said Hill. "Gen. Lee's plan for today was to have Early and Johnson make an early dawn exploratory attack on the hills to the north, followed by Hood's and my attack on the Union's southern line around the Little Round Top."

"We'll have to wait and hear from Gen. Early as to how they did, but after seeing Gen. Lee's condition, we halted our attack plan pending consultation with yourself, or Gen. Lee if he was able. We thought it best to hold off till we had gathered our full forces and consulted with you.

"What did Lee say? Was he conscious at all?" asked Longstreet.

"He seemed delirious," said Hood. "He made no sense. The surgeons both agreed he's had another heart attack and maybe a slight stroke. They said it was best to let him sleep. They thought he wouldn't be in full control of his faculties for awhile, maybe even days."

"You mean he's incapable of command?" Silence. The profundity of the reality struck each of the assembled generals dumb. No one dared to pronounce that conclusion.

"Well. That's that. It seems fate has dealt me this hand, then. Let's review where we stand and what we *do* know until we hear from Early. And Stuart. Whenever that is."

Gen. Longstreet, now in full command, ordered his reserve cavalry units to head for the battle scenes and report back post haste. They went around the table and each expressed his thoughts on waiting for The General to awake and give orders, or in the event he was unable, for Gen. Longstreet to either devise a consensus battle plan, or to try to follow Lee's original plan and improvise as they proceeded, or last option, plan an orderly retreat under cover of the night: slink off like cowards under cover of darkness.

General Hill was the first to speak. "Let us not mention the least likely option. We are here to stand and fight and God willing, to beat this Union army, or in the least to drive it back to its den in Abraham's hovel. For myself and my men, I choose to chastise the Yankees."

"Well said, well said. I'm sure we all share your sentiments, exactly," answered General Hood. "But let us put our minds to the task ahead of us. Let's say General Lee is not able to lead us from his bed. I say we must thoughtfully weigh our strengths and weaknesses and suit them to our enemy's. Where he is weak we must prevail. Where he is strong, we must give way or avoid or neutralize. I know this is not General Lee's methods, and forgive me Gen. Longstreet, but none of us has his ability to improvise on the field. We must play this game with our heads or we will surely lose them."

Longstreet nodded silently. He still awaited the arrival of his immediate subordinate, Gen. George Pickett and several other units, strung out along the Chambersburg Pike west of Gettysburg. Until his force was at full strength he would spend the afternoon weighing the momentous decisions thrust upon him. With the battlefield now strangely quiet, he lit a cigar and stared blankly at his generals. The silent ghost in the somber gathering of hawks, was the white-maned eagle, General Robert E. Lee. And he slept peacefully in his tent nearby, under the watchful eyes of his two doctors.

A Bear up a Tree
Late afternoon, July 2nd

"The two most powerful warriors are Patience and Time"
Leo Tolstoy

Late in the afternoon Major Gen. George Pickett arrived with his First Corps and shortly thereafter Jeb Stuart came in with his cavalry division. Now Gen. Longstreet assembled his generals, including the now battered Jubal A. Early. They discussed the situation on the Union hills and ridges, and the vital Union supply line along the Baltimore Pike. Jeb Stuart added his appraisal of the Union Army of the Potomac he had shadowed for the past three weeks.

"I would estimate their combined strengths at somewhere around 100,000, that's including the cavalry division I ran into back at Brandy Station. Their only weakness that I see is their supply lines, and those I can cut." Polling his generals, Longstreet numbered his assembled Army of Northern Virginia at nearly 69,000. He calculated roughly 3,000 men dead, wounded, captured or missing from the day's action, and guessed at higher Union losses. After an hour of conferring with returning cavalry couriers, and several cups of fortified camp coffee, Gen. Longstreet formally addressed his generals.

"Gentlemen, from everything I've heard I estimate the Union strength up on those hills at close to ninety, maybe as much as 100 thousand. I've been a soldier all my adult life, and I don't recall seeing a stronger defensive position outside an actual fortress. No matter how much we bombard those entrenched positions, no matter how determined our boys are in rushing those hills from flank or front, I know from all my experience it'd take four times our numbers to drive those yanks off those hills. And gentlemen, we just don't have those numbers. Now I know the Commanding General was working out a detailed strategy, which I understand involves renewing yesterday's and today's attack against the Union's flanks. I don't think it'll be any surprise to you that I strongly disagree with any offensive moves against those dug-in positions. Again, I say, we do not have sufficient strength to take the offensive, and even if we did I would never give the order that would sacrifice so many brave young men in storming a fortress. That would pit our weakness against their greater strength. No, gentlemen, *that is NOT MY plan.* No, I say we must play *our strength* against *their weakness.* And what is our strength? We have the beast cornered and we have the option of mobility; he does not. He is locked into a defensive position while we have freedom of movement. *That* is our strength. And his weakness is his supply line, which we must cut off. We can starve him out. We can wait him out, and he can't touch *our* supply lines. That is our strength and that is his weakness. We must not play into Meade's strength. We can control this contest."

"Gentlemen, what do you think we have here?" He stabbed his finger onto the map at the middle of Cemetery Ridge. A satisfied smile creased his lips. "I do believe we've got ourselves *a bear up a tree*. And we've got him surrounded with a bunch of blue tick hounds. That bear ain't got but one place to go, gentlemen... and that's smack dab into our laps. Whaddaya think?"

"That's for sure, not the way The Old Man'd see it," answered Gen. John Hood with a solemn shake of his head. "His plan right away was to attack before they got too dug in. He was waiting for you and Stuart to come in before finalizing the overall plan of attack. Then what, we don't know. Knowing him, something unexpected."

"Plan of attack? *Attack?*" said Longstreet incredulously. Can you all seriously think we can attack 100,000 Union troops dug into a heavily fortified defensive position with our remaining 60,000 infantry plus our 9,500 cavalry? Are we mad men? I hope I don't believe even Gen. Lee would seriously consider a direct attack. No, gentlemen he must have had something else up his sleeve, although God Almighty I can't imagine what he could be thinking."

Right!" said Gen. Early. "Those Yanks *are dug in now,* and I just lost 300 good men trying to drive them off Culp's Hill. That was Gen. Lee's orders, and they had too strong a position to waste more men on it. Maybe we could take it and other fortified hilltops, but it'd cost us too dear a price."

"I agree," said A.P Hill. "We lost too many good Virginians this morning. Military wisdom says we need four men to drive one man off a fortified hill and we can't even match them man for man. I say this ninety degree sun will dry up their water by two to three days and they'll soon eat through their remaining rations. I say we wait for General Sun and General Thirst and General Starvation to take their toll on them dug in Yanks. First, cut that supply line!"

Longstreet now spoke up, "Gentlemen, if we all agree, we'll set up a siege, but with a twist. We'll give them two days in the hot sun.

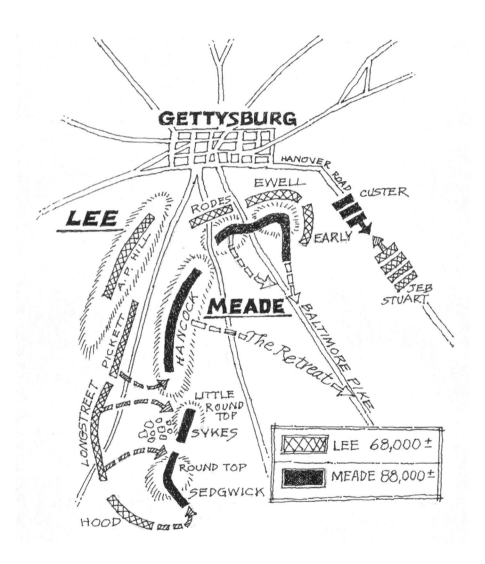

The "Bear in the Tree"

We'll feint attacks on their flanks and hammer their center with all our cannon. If we can turn either flank, Meade may panic and order a retreat. We leave the Baltimore Pike open as their escape route. Then we can ambush and harass them from all sides clear back to Washington, or wherever Meade wants to rest 'em. Time's now on our side and we can stock up on supplies from these rich farmlands. By that time The General should be recovered, God willin', and he can work his magic on their retreat. Now let's set our hounds on 'em and see if we can worry that bear up in the tree."

The Blue Tick Hounds of Old V'ginny
6 A.M. July 3

Corp. Beuford Forrest Ralston stared in amazement at the lieutenant's horse screaming wildly as it galloped away across the open field. Union cannon thundered from the top of Culp's Hill and those deadly canisters of grape shot whistled over Beuford's head as enemy shells burst all around him. He stood fence post still as he gaped at the mortally wounded horse fearfully fleeing the danger all around. Beuford had seen a lung-shot deer bound away for a hundred yards, then stagger and drop dead. He'd seen his deer drop dead when hit, only to jump up and lead him and his hounds on a merry chase through swamp and brambles. But a horse? Jump back up when hit and downed, and gallop till it collapsed? Never seen that before. It all happened so fast, yet it seemed now to flow in slow motion; but it only lasted 10 seconds.

"Stop that horse! *STOP THAT HORSE!*" screamed Beuford. Men were swirling all over the slope of Culp's Hill where the I Corps of the Union army was now hammering Beuford's regiment before the

34

Confederates could overrun the Union position.

Corp. Ralston saw the whole thing in slow motion, dreamlike; the lieutenant riding up to Beuford's company, shouting instructions to the men to wheel left to concentrate the attack on the defenders' extreme fight flank, its weakest point.

Amid the din of battle, an exploding shell had blown apart the lieutenant and mortally wounded his horse. It happened so close to where Beuford was standing the only thing that saved him was the upper half of the lieutenant's body and the entire right side of his horse. The horse stumbled from the impact and fell to its knees before instantly screaming in pain and galloping away, with its rider's legs and waist still upright in the saddle and the half torn away upper torso flopping side to side at a forty-five degree angle as the rocking horse flung it flapping like a severed rag doll.

In the smoke Beuford made out two dim forms in gray jackets throw up their arms and grab the reins as the horse lost its footing and collapsed in front of them. A pistol shot rang out as Beuford ran up to the group, arms and legs of horse and men flailing wildly in the air. Then all seemed deathly quiet as Corp. Ralston and two men of Company D detached the remains of Lt. Livingston from stirrup and saddle. A thunderous crash beside the dead beast and Beuford felt himself lifted out of his shoes as the dawning sky suddenly swirled into blackness.

"Corporal Ralston! Corporal Ralston. Can you hear me?" Beuford half opened his eyes, then winced at the stabbing pain in his right arm, and another in his butt. He groaned and through half-drooped eyelids focused on the white armband with the red cross. It was turning the tourniquet tighter on his arm but it didn't lessen the pain.

"You'll be all right, soldier. I think we can save that arm."

Unknown to Beuford, the attack on the flank had turned the feint into a rout. The entrenched yanks were trapped in their position, and unable to gather enough firepower at the end of their line, had broken ranks and run to the safety of Cemetery Hill. Meade was shaken.

Thunder and Lightning
7:00 A.M., two days later

While Gen. Ewell and Corporal Beuford had shoved the Union's right flank off Culp's Hill, and rattled Gen. Meade, Longstreet had sent Jeb Stuart on a far more important mission. Amid the distraction, Stuart's cavalry had surprised and captured the Union stores and the vital baggage train feeding the beleaguered troops on the hills. Two days without rations and water would give Meade food for thought, reckoned Old Pete. That and two days of 95 degrees.

Old Pete Longstreet's next military strategy was to "shake the bear's tree again." He ordered a heavy artillery barrage against the middle of the Union lines after a feint on both flanks; at Cemetery Hill and simultaneously at the Round Tops. Confederate cannon boomed from 7:00-10:00 am and then fell silent. In the distance a new source of thunder was heard; lightning and rolling thunder heralded an approaching summer storm.

While Meade welcomed the rain as a heaven sent source of water to quench his troops' thirst, he feared what an overabundance might mean to the trenches he'd dug for his divisions. And his rations he reasoned could only last a few more days. Then what?

By noon the storm roared in with full throat. Pete sat in his tent, enjoying the rain and a cigar. His generals joined him.

"Imagine it won't take long for them there entrenchments up on the ridge to fill up with this gully-washer." He smiled at Generals

Hood, Stuart and Pickett. His entire force now held their positions and waited for General Rain and General Hunger to soak and starve the Union Army.

Old Pete Longstreet's strategy was playing out as hoped. He had ordered a merciless cannonade against the middle of the Union Line where he felt it would do the most damage. For several hours he had directed a pounding of the Union positions atop Cemetery Ridge. He had withdrawn Hood's division on the extreme Union left at Big Round Top after an early morning feint. He left an open path to the Baltimore Pike for the ever cautious and wary Meade, if so inclined.

The early morning feints on Cemetery Hill and Big Round Top together with the artillery barrage served notice to Meade that the rebels now controlled the battle. If Old Pete's tactics proved effective, it was only a matter of time before a wet and hungry Union army saw the hopelessness of holding onto their mud-filled entrenchments while waiting for the enemy's next move. Or until hunger forced Meade to attempt a strategic retreat. He could not help but note that the Confederates had failed to close the route to the Baltimore Pike all along the rear of his positions. But he waited for the rain to let up. It didn't. The summer thunderstorm continued on into the night and into the next morning. Meade had only two choices now, and he dreaded them both.

Apres Lee, le Deluge
July 6, 1863

Gen. Robert E. Lee awoke around 6 a.m. the morning of July 6th. A strange quiet greeted him. No booming of cannon. No whistling of canisters of lead hornets. No neighing of nervous horses. No crackling of a thousand muskets and smooth bore rifles. Then he heard a sound sweet to his memory; a reel, a Virginia mountain reel. Somewhere nearby, a single violin bowed out the haunting strains of a beloved Shenandoah reel. A lad from Corporal Beuford Ralston's Fortieth Virginia Volunteer Infantry Regiment was playing a familiar tune for his company buddy who'd received a serious shrapnel wound in his butt during the fight on Culp's Hill. Though the tune was meant for Beuford, lying painfully in the infirmary tent, the fluid notes were just as sweet to his equally prone Commander-in-Chief lying in his own tent next to Corporal Ralston's infirmary tent. As Gen. Lee stirred in bed, his physicians came over to him.

"You're looking much better, sir. You had yourself a good sleep!"

"How long have I been unconscious?"

"In and out of consciousness, off and on for four days, sir. We thought we'd lost you there for a while. You've had a heart attack and maybe a mild stroke. We felt it was best to keep you sedated. Sleep is a great healer. Your color's come back now. How do you feel, sir?"

"I'd like to get out of bed. I need to see my generals."

"Better for them to come to you. Shall I send for Gen. Longstreet? He took over the command while you rested."

"They can't see me like this. I'd like to get dressed." The two doctors exchanged glances and nodded.

"Yes, sir. We think you're sufficiently recovered. You can get into your uniform. But best to take it easy till you've had a good breakfast."

The patient smiled. Breakfast. When had he last eaten? No memory. Suddenly he was very hungry.

"That would be a welcome treat, doctor."

Then over the lilting bars of the reel, Lee heard another beautiful sound; it was raining on the tent. The storm was now a softly pattering summer shower, accompanied by a change of tune to a Virginia waltz.

By the time an aide delivered a breakfast of grits, ham and coffee, the morning shower changed back to a steady rain, and distant thunder threatened to drown out Beuford's serenade. By the time Lee's tent was filled with a dozen of his generals, the rain threatened to resume its full-fledged gully washer strength.

General James Old Pete Longstreet waited for his commander to speak first. The gathered chair-bound generals searched The Old Man's face and were relieved to see that General Robert Lee had definitely returned to the land of the living. Ham and grits had restored a healthy glow to his face and his cheeks were almost rosy above the neatly clipped gray beard.

"Well, General Longstreet, how have we done? Did you follow my battle plan or did you improvise? How did Meade greet your invitation to the dance?"

Longstreet was equally chastised by the "improvisation" which he was definitely not expected to do, as well as he was pleased that not only did he fail to follow Lee's daringly risky battle strategy, but he had outwitted the Union Army in his own way, or rather with the consensus revised battle plan of his subordinate generals.

Gen. Meade had chosen not to fight his way off the hills and risk losing more men in a confrontation. Under the cover of night, he had ordered a strategic retreat out the "back door"-- down the wide open Baltimore Pike. If he thought he could save the greater part of his army to fight another day and rob Lee of a victory or God forbid a total surrender, then wary, cautious, deliberate Meade was in for a shock. Somewhere down the Baltimore Pike, Gen. Pickett waited with 12,500 fresh troops. A little further, flanking the pike in dense woods waited Gen. A.P. Hill with another 15,000 veterans of Chancellorsville.

30,000 Confederate infantry and Jeb Stuart's cavalry were waiting to harass the rear guard of Meade's retreating corps, with orders not to confront the main body of the Union army. Longstreet's strategy was to harass and run, follow and chew on the stragglers, and to reduce Gen. Meade's force piecemeal without committing to pitched battles. If Meade chose to stand and fight, the pursuers were to wait for Gen. Lee's recovery and let the Commanding General dictate the course of action.

The Army of Northern Virginia had lost 7,000 men in five days of battle against entrenched Union troops and Lee could not afford a battle of attrition. Better to let a battered Union Army of the Potomac retreat back across the Potomac and face their political and editorial critics. That howling mob would do as much to unsettle the Northern war mongers as an outright defeat administered by the Army of Northern Virginia. Lee did not need a total victory at Gettysburg to achieve his objectives in his Northern Campaign.

General James Old Pete Longstreet explained his actions to his recuperating Commander in Chief:

"Sir, we've rattled the fox out of his den and have him on the run. Meade's strung out for fifteen miles south along the Baltimore Pike and we have Stuart running him hard with Pickett and Hill waiting in ambush. Not a very elegant strategy, but it's cost us next to nothing in our men's lives and we've captured the bulk of his supplies and many stragglers."

"You mean there was no fight? He just packed up and ran? We had him surrounded, how'd he escape?"

"You might say we let him go. But instead of confronting him in his trenches, we battered him with cannon. But it was the rain, mud and lost rations that drove him off the hills. We left an avenue open for him to escape. His retreat will cost him dearly while we harry him all the way to Baltimore, or even back to Washington. He'll be lucky to field even half as many troops as he came to town with."

Lee was not pleased. His goal was to crush the Army of the Potomac where they were. His men felt invincible. They'd do anything he asked of them. Why had Longstreet let Meade go? They'd almost had the Yanks after that first day. All he had to do was attack and drive them off the hills. Meade would have collapsed. They would have had a total and complete victory. Now the enemy would stumble back across the Potomac and into the safety of either Baltimore or Washington. They'd live to face Lee's army another day, another Gettysburg. Damn! But he could not chastise his generals publicly for what Lee saw as their shortcomings. That was up to Providence. Better to work on a bold strategy to catch the foe with his back to the Potomac and crush him there.

"We'll see, men. We'll see. Please gather with me at lunch and we'll see where we go from here. We may trap that cautious fox yet, before he finds another den."

General Mud & General Rain
July 7, 1863

Gen. Jeb Stuart sat his horse in the woods along the Baltimore Pike, still in Pennsylvania but near the Maryland border. The soggy procession he was watching was a miserable mob of infantry and artillery companies strung out nearly fifteen miles. He had watched them all morning as they labored in the steady downpour, ankle deep in mud, horses and mules already nearly exhausted from the punishing battle with General Mud and General Rain. Stuart had dispatched a rider back to Lee with a summary of what he'd witnessed the past six hours since daylight. The Grand Army of the Potomac had found their way out of a trap Meade thought, to carry out a successful strategic retreat down the Baltimore Pike under cover of darkness. Meade supposed that Lee was too battered to pursue, or was gathering his forces for another attack. Whatever Lee's intentions, Meade himself counted his losses in five day's fighting at nearly 12,000. He calculated three more days or more at that rate and he'd have lost 20% of his command. And if Lee persisted in his attacks, he would have paid too dearly also. Either way, there could be no victory at that rate for either army. He must limp back to the safety of Baltimore and refill his rosters to full strength. He would live to fight Lee another day, at another place.

The courier handed Stuart's note to Gen. Lee's adjutant. The Old Man was dressed for action, but resting in his tent under orders from his doctors. Lee read Jeb Stuart's words and thoughtfully stroked his beard. An entirely new strategy suddenly flooded into "Marse Robert's" nimble brain. He called for his adjutant to summon his generals. While Meade prayed for the rain to let up, Stuart and Lee called upon the Gods of Thunder and Lightning to keep it coming.

"Gentlemen," said Lee with a pleased look crossing his newly rosy face, "I do believe the Almighty has presented us with an opportunity for a most welcome victory." He laid out the map showing the Baltimore Pike running straight southeast from Gettysburg to Baltimore. He pointed out the positions of the waiting corps of Pickett and Hill, poised to pounce on the flanks of the overextended Union Army. "It seems this heavy, constant rain has slowed Meade's march to a miserable crawl. They're only making two miles every hour in that muddy road and he can't push them much further without a day's rest. The nearest town is Westminster, right here, twenty miles from his vanguard units. He can't get there even in a hard day's ten hour march. But before that he'll have to strike a bargain with Hill and Pickett. Gentlemen I believe the Good Lord has laid victory in our lap. Here's my thought. I'll give Jeb Stuart a note from me asking Meade to spare us from unnecessarily grinding down his battalions on the way to Baltimore. I will give Gen. Meade the sensible option for a conditional surrender. I fully expect his generals to refuse. We then enfilade his stalled column from front, sides and rear simultaneously. I would expect them to see the hopelessness of their situation and come to terms. If they refuse, God help them, they are dead men marching to Hell."

Lee's generals were stunned. This wasn't the Gen. Lee they knew. He was advocating a guerrilla warfare tactic of hit and run, ambush and retreat; a slow death of attrition for his adversary. It was the simple strategy of the Minutemen harassing the retreating British column on the Concord Road. And to a man, they wholeheartedly saw the wisdom of the strategy, most especially as long as the rain continued to slow Meade's progress. Now, the question was at what point did The General propose to hand Meade this ultimatum?

"As for the opportune timing, I propose to bring both Pickett and Hill against their vanguard this afternoon, before Meade can set up a defense and before his tired men can rest. We can batter them and demoralize them by simultaneously hitting them in the rear with Stuart's cavalry. Then we withdraw, let them consider their precarious position and deliver my ultimatum for Meade's complete surrender. Any thoughts, gentlemen?" Lee stood straight as a pine, hands folded behind his back, resplendent in his freshly laundered and brushed field uniform.

The assembled generals looked at each other and exchanged assuring nods of approval. They felt the heavens had opened at the most propitious time and the Goddess of Victory had handed them her laurel branch.

The Quagmire
4 p.m July 7, 1863

"What a cruel thing is war; to separate and destroy families and friends ... to fill our hearts with hatred instead of love for our neighbors, and to devastate the fair face of this beautiful world."
                    Robert E. Lee, letter to his wife, 1864

Private Alfred Werner Swanson of the 142nd N.Y. Regiment had slogged in muddy roads many a time urging the oxen to haul the great white pine logs down through the springtime muddy logging roads outside Frewsburg, N.Y. He and his sturdy lumberjack crew had chopped down one of the tallest stands of virgin white pine in the entire northeast. The harvested lumbered would be rafted down the Conewango to the junction of the Allegheny and on the spring flood all the way to Pittsburgh. Now here in southeastern Pennsylvania, this muddy track called the Baltimore Pike was no different than Frew Run's logging trail after an all night gully washer.

Unfortunately for Private Swanson and his Regiment, they were in the vanguard of the 80,000 survivors of the retreat from Gettysburg. About 4:00 in the afternoon of July 7, Swanson heard the rumble of thunder ahead. Strange how it sounded just like the thunder of artillery his eardrums had been tortured by, a scant five days earlier. Suddenly the rolling thunder was accompanied by exploding shells just ahead of him, shredding members of the first company in the vanguard unit. He dove for the ditch as his captain shouted the order to take cover.

"Damn it! We're a bunch of sittin' ducks," swore Swanson to the men in the ditch beside him. He felt like a duck; half underwater in a muddy ditch alongside the thick woods flanking the Baltimore Pike. The incessant rain had hammered him with no letup, all day. And now, enemy cannon fire exploding ahead of, to the side of and then a terrific boom in the road where his column had slogged moments ago. Private Swanson shook with the concussion and suddenly was aware of a new sensation: a wet warmth spread along the crotch of his pants. He instantly knew he'd been hit and waited for the antici-pated shock of pain from the shrapnel. But there wasn't any; his wound was of the self-inflicted kind, caused by a sudden emotional trauma.

"Damn!" He swore at himself as he realized he'd wet his pants. Then a long sigh of relief, relief of the other kind as he realized it could have been worse--and more embarrassing. There would be no relief for his142nd till dark silenced the Confederate artillery bom-bardment. Private Swanson would have to huddle in the muddy ditch for six more wet, dreary hours. Since his regiment's retreat from the crest of Cemetery Hill, they had covered the tortuous distance of six-teen miles down the muddy Baltimore Pike in a full two days of re-lentless rain, and now continuous bombardment by an unseen enemy.

A blood-curdling scream and a chorus of moans from the ditch twenty yards down the road told Private Swanson his wet pants were a cheap price exacted on him by the Gods of War. Up ahead, where the shell exploded, the unlucky men of his company lay stunned or shredded depending on which kind of shells hit them. Alfred and three of his ditch-mates stumbled ahead to assess the damage; the sight made him turn his head away, his stomach convulsing up into his mouth. He launched his lunch into the bushes. "Oh! Jee-zus! Them bastards! Oh, Christ, what have you done?" It was all he could say, repeating the words over and over as he reached down to try to help one of his best friends, who moaned and clutched the remains of his tunic front where his stomach used to be. Private Swanson turned away and wrenched his guts again at the sight of his friend Jesse's red-gushing gut wound.

Earlier in the day, Private Swanson and Jesse had talked about the rumors sweeping their regiment. Word spread that Confederate infantry and artillery lay in ambush all the way to Winchester. They knew they'd pay hell before they reached the safety of Winchester, let alone Meade's Baltimore haven. Then, too, as Private Alfred Swanson repeated to his friend, Lee had offered them a generous surrender.

"Surrender! Hell!" snorted Jessee. "I'll die with my rifle in hand before I'll ever surrender to them damn traitor rebs!"

Before the kneeling medic could shove a swath of bandage into the gaping wound, Jesse's eyes rolled heavenward and his head slumped onto his chest. The War God had fulfilled another defiant warrior's wish. Private Swanson stared, stunned at the reality of war that lay around him in the ditch and the edge of the woods. "If that shell had come just another twenty yards..." He couldn't comprehend the conclusion; his mind was numb. "What am I doing here?" he thought. "Where's the glory? There's no damn Glory!"

His next reaction was a grumbling anger; the pent-up frustration from the realization that his unit could be obliterated in the mud at any random moment. He might die in a ditch. So much for the glory of war. His thoughts were interrupted by the captain shouting out a new order: "Take cover in the woods! Get behind those big trees!"

Suddenly, Private Swanson felt a surge of calmness, as though an old friend had reached down and offered a helping hand. Big trees. The woods on the side of the Baltimore Pike were a thick stand of maple, oak and tulip with a preponderance of giant chestnuts. Big trees akin to the giant white pines of his native Chautauqua hills. He felt their welcoming presence as he knelt by the trunk of a large chestnut tree. Different trees, same sense of wonder and awe at the thick old bodies that shielded his fragile company from the unseen Confederate artillery.

"Men, I want four squads to either side of the pike. You're going to go get those Rebel batteries and blow them to kingdom come before they annihilate us here." The Captain barked his orders.

Private Swanson fell in with the point, led by Corporal Hendrix. They jogged from tree to tree until they saw a low cloud of smoke hanging over the pike and spreading into their side of the woods. "God's taken our side, boys!" whispered Corporal Hendrix as he hand signaled the squad to fix bayonets. "We'll circle them and charge from the rear on my signal. But wait till they're busy reloading." It seemed like a logical plan. But in war, logic often watches from the sidelines.

No sooner were they in position to the flank of the artillery drawn up in the center of the road, than the two squads on the far side of the pike began to fire. Almost simultaneously, a company of Rebel infantry, drawn up behind the cannon as a shield, answered with a withering fire. Corporal Hendrix quickly decided against the bayonet charge and ordered an enfilade from the cover of the big trees. The Rebels were caught in a deadly cross-fire, but instead of breaking and running they let out their wild high-pitched yell and charged Swanson's squad.

Everything now swirled madly in slow motion. Private Swanson saw Hendrix go down with a bloody face as two gray-clad figures bounded out of the knee-deep layer of cannon smoke. Men were screaming and swearing, shooting and clubbing with their rifle butts. Swanson watched as his bayonet slashed a short arch and nearly beheaded a charging rebel while a second was flung backward from the blast of a rifle close to Swanson's shoulder. In what may have been thirty seconds but seemed like thirty minutes, a swirl of slashing, charging rebel infantry were cut down by Private Swanson's squad and their supporting squad.

Swanson stared down at the Corporal. He lay motionless, one leg bent as if to kick, arms spread and his face a mask of blood. He would give no more orders. A voice to the left said, "I think you're next in command, Swanson." He turned dumbly towards the voice and the face. The remnants of his squad stood questioningly. What now? Swanson heard a hoarse voice rasp, "Fix bayonets! We charge those bastards! No quarter!" The voice was his and his legs were churning through the the tall, wet grass lining the pike's ditch. Again the battle rage choked his senses and he was only aware of men clubbing, slashing, spinning, falling, bleeding, swearing and groaning as both his squad and his companion squads danced a death quadrille with the rebel artillerymen.

Swanson's ears echoed with the booming of close-range pistol and rifle talk. Then he was aware of the complete silence. He looked at the still cannon, standing expectantly in the middle of the Baltimore Pike as if to say, I'm ready, what are we waiting for? But there was no one left to light their wicks or feed their muzzles their next iron meal.

Private Swanson stood bewildered among the remains of their four squadrons. He did not grasp the full meaning of what had just been done. Only fifteen men were still standing, mostly unscathed. They and Private Swanson were the lucky ones. The Goddess of War had chosen to protect and preserve these lucky few with her mantle of mercy. They knew they were not heroes, just survivors. Now what? They looked at each other, then they all stared at Private Alfred Swanson. "I think you're still in charge, Alf. Everyone else is dead. Almost. Corporal Graham's hurt bad. What d'ya wanna do?"

He took a deep breath. "First, let's turn these damn cannon the other way. We might have visitors any minute. Jones, run back fast as you can and tell Jackson, Captain Jackson, to git the hell up here with artillery men and cavalry fast's he can. The rest of you post behind the trees either side and git ready for another fight. I suspect we'll have a hornet's nest of rebs on our necks real soon. And grab all the rifles and cartridges you find. We're gunna need 'em!" He motioned his hand and led half the men into the woods.

It seemed like an hour, but it wasn't. No sooner had they huddled into defensive positions behind the shielding trunks than they heard horses clumping towards them from the south.

"Here they come! Fire when they reach the cannon." The far woods erupted first. Private Swanson had behaved like a Private; he forgot to arrange a strategy and a signal. Now it would be every man for himself. The Union men's new Sharps repeaters spit out their deadly firestorm and the first ranks of rebel cavalry fell. The following column wheeled and collided in a scramble to ride to safety. Swanson heard a rider yell "Ambush!" The horse soldiers knew instinctively what to do; flee to safety out of range.

As the drumming of retreating hooves tapered down the pike, it was echoed by thumping boots from the advancing Union vanguard; Jones and the reinforcements. Private Swanson let out a deep sigh of relief. He was suddenly aware of an uncontrollable shaking of his rifle hand. It felt like some unseen soldier, or his ghost, was either shaking his hand and arm or trying to loosen his grip on his gunstock. He grabbed his right wrist with his left and squeezed hard. The ghost let go.

No sooner had he controlled his shaking hands than a cold sweat broke over his forehead. No, it wasn't the mist or the rain. He'd seen cases of shell shock. Was he one? He gritted his teeth and fought to control himself. Then the relief column was here.

The tall, slim Captain dismounted in one fluid move and looked at the muddy riflemen assembled by the cannon. "What happened here? Who's in command?"

"Me, Sir," saluted Private Swanson. "We took their artillery and beat off their relief."

"And who the hell are you, Private? Where's your corporal?"

"Dead, Sir. They're all dead." A complete and detached calm now settled on Private Swanson. "I took command, Captain Jackson, Sir. Private Alfred Swanson." The captain stared into the mud spattered face that answered his questions and a faint smirk turned the corners of his mouth. "Private Swanson. Swanson? Alfred Swanson, 142nd Jamestown Infantry Regiment?" He walked slowly up to the muddy soldier and stared him down. There was no flinching response from a soldier who had just killed how many rebels he didn't know, and whose battle shock had been replaced with a steady calmness rooted in the relief that the War Gods had chosen to spare him.

"Private Swanson. You are now Corporal Swanson. Take your command and rejoin your regiment in the vanguard. I'll need a full report later."

David & Goliath--
A Glorious Charge
July 7, 1863

The morning rain dripped off the wide brim of his black velvet hat. His horse's flanks glistened from the steady wetness of the scudding clouds racing overhead. George sat his horse as if they were part of each other. Their six legs were all part of the same creature; a modern day centaur. When they galloped over the fields of battle, nostrils snorting, eyes wide and flashing, long manes flying in the wind, and hooves thundering in demonic rhythm, George imagined himself the very God of War himself. Ironically, the merest bullet from a lowly coward's rifle would have been enough to end the egotistical fantasy of General George Armstrong Custer.

George Armstrong Custer had been promoted from a captain to Brevet Brigadier General after his dashing heroics against Confederate cavalry at Brandy Station and Beverly Ford on the Rappahanock on June 9. He was a brash twenty-three-year-old 1861 graduate of West Point, a rowdy goof-off whose long list of demerits dropped his otherwise good grades down to a rank of thirty-four in a graduating class of thirty-four. Nevertheless, George was a promising army prospect; he favored audacious, reckless battle tactics, traits that were to send his fortunes rocketing like a meteor in the military skies to come. In spite of his questionable military acumen, George was first and foremost a horseman.

His nemesis was a battle-hardened cavalry genius, the thirty-year-old veteran, General Jeb Stuart, whose Confederate cavalry division of around 9,500 troopers had earned the nickname "The Invincibles." No Union cavalry had yet gained a victory over Stuart's Invincibles. It was only a matter of time before the brash twenty-three-year-old Custer tested his tactics against the thirty-year-old veteran cavalryman's Invincibles.

Custer's time and place of destiny arrived on the late morning of July 7 on the Baltimore Pike, twelve miles south of Gettysburg. After hooking up with Lee, late on the 2nd of July, Stuart had discussed a bold attack plan with his commander. Shortly after, Gen. Lee suffered his latest mild heart attack and his battle plan was put on hold by Gen. Longstreet who now took over Lee's command function. Longstreet was vehemently opposed to Lee's rash plan of attack as told privately to only Stuart and Lee's three Corps commanders. Longstreet made the cautious decision not to follow the boldest moves of Lee's battle plan. That left Jeb Stuart idly waiting for either a new plan from Longstreet or best case for Jeb, Lee's revival and implementation of his original plan.

Now, late in the morning of July 7, while Meade's army slogged along the pike in a muddy retreat, Stuart led 6,000 of his cavalry troops towards the rear guard of Meade's army. The only part of the Union Army that had not been hit by Pickett and Hill's ambushing artillery were the cavalry units under Gen. David Gregg, now guarding the rear of Meade's XI Corps. Leading the Fifth Michigan cavalry brigade was twenty-three-year-old George Armstrong Custer. Gregg's total cavalry strength was 4,400 plus a column of XI Corps infantry in addition to Custer's 2,400 man brigade.

Being advised that Confederate cavalry had been spotted behind them on the pike, Custer knew the rebels were about to test the Union rear guard. Even if it was just a reconnaissance probe, Custer was itching to test his battle stars against The Invincibles. Jealousy and ambition gnawed at his ego. He was ready to ride, ready to charge. He asked Gen. Gregg for permission to place his Fifth Michigan brigade in the extreme rear, in position to thwart the brunt of Stuart's anticipated attack. Gregg was only too happy to let his green junior take the first hit. It came quickly.

Custer arranged his brigade on the muddy Baltimore Pike in squadrons of six horses wide by seventeen deep, two lengths between from tail to nose. He then spaced his companies six lengths apart and stacked them almost a quarter mile back so as to fill the roadway with his entire brigade. Lastly he placed two companies of 100 infantry, armed with repeating Sharps rifles in the woods on either side of the road. Now he was ready to spring his trap for the unsuspecting Invincibles. He ordered his lieutenants to wait for his signal to charge. Then he ceremoniously unsheathed his saber and cantered away back up the Baltimore Pike to await the appearance of the lead company of Jeb Stuart's Invincibles.

George Custer had a history of flamboyance, in manner and appearance. He wanted his men to see him as a bold, fearless and distinguished leader. And so he dressed accordingly. His hat was a wide-brimmed black velvet with one brim tied up to the side. He topped it off with an ostrich plume. His field jacket was replaced with a showy black velvet coat trimmed with elaborate gold braid. His boots were a knee length cavalier style better fitted for the French Musketeers than the Union cavalry. To demonstrate his audacity he rode at the head of his column in full sight of the approaching enemy. His manner instilled an esprit de corps in the Fifth Michigan like no other unit in the Union cavalry.

As if on cue, down the pike came Stuart's first squadron. As they rounded the bend they were surprised to see a lone horseman, dressed like a circus rider, waiting for them in the rain. They halted and stared, not sure what to make of the strange apparition. Before they could decide what to do next, the flamboyant rider whirled his saber high above his head and spurred his horse, charging straight at them. Fifty paces away he wheeled and yelled a curse at them and galloped back down the pike. Immediately the lead squadron chased after him. Before they realized they were being led into an ambush, a withering rifle fire cut the lead squadron to pieces.

Now Custer did the completely unexpected. He yelled at his men, "Michigan men! Follow me!" And he charged ahead into the retreating survivors of the Confederate cavalry. Stuart's column now met their retreating men crashing into their halted horsemen with Union cavalry in heated pursuit. Within minutes the lead squads of Stuart's Invincibles were in furious hand-to- hand saber fights with a swarming Fifth Michigan, which then broke off and galloped back to their waiting formation blocking the Baltimore Pike, shielding the retreating Union rear guard.

The Confederates quickly regrouped and comprehended the bold plan of the blocking Union cavalry. They would have to cut through squadron after squadron, ninety men against ninety men until one or the other group ran out of pawns. Numbers on either side no longer mattered; this narrow battlefield only allowed a six-horse-wide team at a time to confront its opponent.

As Jeb Stuart rode through his lines to assess the roadblock, he was quick to appreciate the brilliance of his opponent's strategy. It was the exact same strategy Leonidas and his 300 Spartans employed against the Persians at Thermopylae. Stuart decided not to play Xerxes against Custer's Leonidas and ordered his troops to pull back for infantry support. For his part, Custer chose to hold his position and simply block the road until the time he expected Stuart to bring up artillery to clear the path. Meanwhile he would employ his blocking stratagem all the way to Baltimore if necessary. For now, his pride glowed in the satisfaction of knowing that he and his Fifth Michigan had beaten back The Invincibles.

The Ultimatum
July 8, 1863

"During times of peace, sons bury their fathers;
in times of war, it is the father who buries his son."

Herodotus

In spite of Gen. Custer's stunning success in stalemating Jeb Stuart's harassment of Meade's rear guard, nothing in the Union Army's bag of tricks could prevent the piecemeal destruction of the Grand Army of the Potomac as it marched in a 15 mile long, vulnerable column towards the anticipated safety of Baltimore. Before he reached the relative safety of Westminster, Gen. Meade had received and rejected Gen. Lee's generous offer of terms for the complete surrender of the Army of the Potomac. But during two more days on the march, with one more to go before reaching Westminster, Meade's retreating 80,000 had been reduced to 65,000 able troops, but with many more wounded than his wagon train could humanely accommodate. It was this fact of confronting the growing misery of his dying and wounded that finally forced Gen. Meade's hand. Beyond the disgrace of surrendering his army, he could not live with the guilt of more blood on his hands. On July 9 at 5:00 in the afternoon, a mere eight hours from Westminster with an unknown number of Confederate artillery raining canisters and shells into his vanguard, and probable ambushes waiting along the road, Gen. George Meade accepted Gen. Robert E. Lee's generous terms of surrender. Meade got to keep his sword, but not his reputation and his dignity.

Old Pete Longstreet's cautious battle strategy had worked magnificently. Marse Robert was left to wonder what would have been the outcome of his grand plan of four arms squeezing the Union men off the Hills of their Gettysburg fortress. Never mind, he now had a larger target in his sights: Washington and President Lincoln.

The road to the Northern Capital was now clear. Lee would rush his army to the outskirts of Washington and threaten to shell the Capital. He would sue for a treaty guaranteeing independence for the Confederate States. He would offer peace; before Generals Grant, Sherman and Sheridan could come to the rescue. He sent urgent orders to Gen. Johnston in Tennessee to block the victors of Vicksburg from reaching Washington in time. Time and the tide were now on the side of the South.

A NEW NATION

The Hounds of The Press
July 12, 1863

The headlines in the Richmond and Charleston newspapers spoke a totally different story than the Baltimore, Philadelphia and New York City papers. So did Washington, D.C.'s, where the citizens cowered in anticipation of an invading Gray Horde, while the politicians including the President and his family prepared to board ships waiting to remove them to the safety of Philadelphia or New York City.

One side howled and railed against the incompetence of Lincoln and his choice of generals, barely mentioning Grant's recent stunning victory at Vicksburg. The Southern press gloried in its praise of the military genius of its favorite son and his brave warriors. But none of this rhetoric, North or South really mattered in the course of events now unfolding. There was a larger piece on the chess board.

In parliament, the House of Lords and the House of Commons debated the fate of the Union and the Confederate cause. Ultimately it was the outcome of this tonsorial battle that would decide whether Lee would have to face Grant in a long drawn-out battle of attrition of soldiers' lives on future battlefields. And in that balance also hung the ultimate fate of three-and-a-half million African slaves south of the Mason-Dixon line. Finally it was the price of a bale of cotton that would tip the English hand one way or the other.

Parliament and King Cotton
September 1, 1863

As soon as the news of Lee's victory at Gettysburg and the surrender of the Army of the Potomac resounded in the newspapers of
Europe and Great Britain, the die was cast. The House of Lords had
already decided that their factories must have Confederate cotton or
their fortunes would stagnate. If the armies of the Northern states
prevailed, cotton supplies would falter and prices would go through
the roof. And so, when the debate in Parliament was over, London
newspapers blared the bold headline under the banner head:

England Recognizes Confederate States of America
A New Separate and Free Nation

President Lincoln countered the threatened collapse of the Union
with renewed calls for more recruits and the urgent recall of Gen.
Grant and the western army to the defense of Washington. It was too
late. The arrival of Grant, Sheridan and Sherman was delayed for
two months by the heroic efforts of a dogged Army of Tennessee led
by Gen. Johnston. Two months after Gettysburg was not enough to
turn the tide of Northern sentiment whirling throughout Ohio, New
Jersey and New York where Lincoln's political adversaries were rallying around the calls of George McClellan for at least a truce and
then a cessation of hostilities. The New Yorkers especially were tired
of the cost of the war effort, aided by McClellan's assertions that Lee
and the Confederate army even if defeated on a conventional battlefield would melt into the countryside and continue the war in a pro-
longed guerrilla mode a la Colonel Mosby's dreaded Rangers. The

price of victory over the South, claimed the New Yorkers was too high. Better to let them ride out their own inevitable storm of slave protest and rebellion. Let *Time* tame the South.

The storm in Congress was swift and decisive. Congress fought among themselves; the lesser states argued in vain against the power of the populous states of Ohio, Pennsylvania, New Jersey and New York. They turned against Lincoln according to their own interests. A long drawn out guerrilla war would bankrupt them they argued. And so two months after Gettysburg a truce was proposed. A month later the Northern half of the United states recognized the Southern half's right to self government. Lincoln's Great Struggle to save the Union was over.

It had been the crushing news from London, that stiffened the political winds in Washington. It was a storm that would wash President Lincoln and his supporters out of Washington. One year later, Gen. George McClellan and *his* supporters would be swept into office in the election of 1864 on a tidal wave of promises to voters of every persuasion.

A Hollow Rhetoric
November 19, 1863

"Only the dead have seen the end of war."

Plato

Five months after the Battle of Gettysburg, Abraham Lincoln sat down in a room in the village of Gettysburg to edit the final touches in the brief speech he was set to deliver; after the keynote speaker at the dedication of the new battlefield cemetery was finished. Abraham Lincoln was a polished wordsmith and he chose each word with great care. As a practiced politician, he had become an eloquent speaker, and his carefully selected words often carried a profound weight. Now he had come to help dedicate this national cemetery on the battlefield where only five months earlier 25,000 soldiers had successfully slaughtered each other. Remnants of the horrific clash were still strewn on the raw, scarred earth; bits of uniforms, equipment and decaying horse skeletons. The November weather added its shroud of gloom to the sad occasion.

The heavy sadness that hung over Gettysburg that day was reflected in the person of the President of the Northern half of the sundered union. He had the tired face of one who had shouldered the burdens of the country and lost much sleep in the effort, and now endured the final defeat of his determined battle to preserve the Union at all costs. His rivals had reckoned the costs as too dear. His previous resolve was now dissolved. His war was over.

Now he selected his final words, pencil in hand on a page of bluish stationary. He would utter only 250 words after U.S. Senator Edward Everett's two-hour oration. Anyone who took a coffee break or took a quick whiz after Everett's marathon would surely miss the President's brief two-minute speech.

What he said that day could be said to be divinely inspired; but it could not be said to be a realistic reflection of his nation's brief history or even of the times, however heartfelt Lincoln's words. This is part of what he said:

*"Four score and seven (87) years ago, our fathers brought forth on this continent, a new nation, **conceived in Liberty**, and dedicated to the proposition that **all men are created equal...".***

Equality was at the heart of the great debate in the halls of Congress at Philadelphia when Benjamin Franklin failed to convince the other forefathers of the nation that slavery was the dark issue that must be resolved sooner or later or it would tear the nation apart. But it was not only slavery and the Afro-American equality issue that required a fair resolution in order to cleanse the soul of the New Republic; women were also not equal in the laws of the Republic. Neither were the civilized (but slave-owning) Cherokees, nor other native Americans. Nor were the recent gold-seeking Chinese immigrants in California. Nor the Mexicans who preceded the Anglos in taking Texas from the Comanches and the Southern Cheyenne.

The Cherokee and their other Five Civilized Tribes of the southeast had suffered the wrath of General Jackson and the scorn of their new European neighbors and were driven from their homeland. In order to justify the legal theft of the natives' lands, the U.S. Supreme court had to declare the Cherokee legally non-humans, non-equals, and therefore the Republic's laws did not protect them.

For his part, Lincoln who in his earlier days as an Illinois militiaman had participated in the removal of the Sauk and Fox from their homeland was not much more equality minded than Jackson. Did Abraham Lincoln consider all these assaults against pure justice when he spoke his careful and precise words at the Gettysburg cemetery? Did it occur to him that certain of his words would ring false and sour just a few generations later? The descendants of Red Jacket, Massasoit, Powhatan, Osceola, Gall and Crazy Horse, Chief Joseph and Geronimo would choke and scoff at some of Abraham Lincoln's paraphrased words of the Founding Fathers as proclaimed by their slave-owning Virginian scribe of 1776.

Yet in another presidential act, Abraham Lincoln would take a profound step towards a more just and fair community of the equally-born inhabitants of the now fragmented nation. He would soon take a long stride in that direction when he officially announced the Federal policy of Freedom for all slaves.... *those within his juris-*

diction. In that effort he would in some measure redeem the soul of the Republic and its declared if not practiced principles. But at the cemetery in Gettysburg, Lincoln's rhetoric did not reflect the reality of either the past or the present. Whether it would match the *future* reality was yet to be decided. Would "that nation, ... so conceived and so dedicated...that government of the people, by the people, for the people..." would that nation perish from the earth? The truth of Lincoln's high-minded words would be tested through coming generations, both in North and South.

A Promise of Freedom
1864

"The time is now at hand which must determine whether we are to be freemen or remain slaves; whether we are to have any property we can call our own. The fate of our unborn millions will now depend on our courage and our conduct in this conflict. Our cruel and unrelenting enemy leaves us only the choice of brave resistance, or submission to chains. We have, therefore, to resolve to be free or die trying."

Paraphrase from July 2, 1776
writings of Geo. Washington

"Hallelujah! Hallelujah! Hallelujah!" The excited shouts rang out in the small cabin that housed the twenty-odd parishioners of the African Zion Baptist Church of Wheylon Bridge, Georgia, a hundred-odd miles north of the Florida boundary. The Reverend Alouyshious Ezekiel "Zeke" Carter had just announced the long-awaited news that President Lincoln had finally issued his proclamation freeing the slaves.

"Now just hold on a minute," warned Reverend Zeke. "Jus' cuz Father Abraham tells us we's free don't mean we can walk out that door free as the breeze. Don't mean no such thing to our masters. They still own every last man, woman and child of us. We got us a long road ahead of us. Long and dangerous."

"Amen, brother, amen!" shouted Joshua Tobias with a shake of his fist.

"Yessuh! Yessuh, Joshua," answered Rev. Zeke. "Father Abraham means well, but he's just talking for our brothers up North. His arm can't reach us all the ways down here in Wheylon Bridge. Or nowhere else for that matter where he don't got no Union soldiers. He ain't got what they calls jurisdiction south of the Mason-Dixon. No suh, brothers and sisters, we got us a long, hard row to hoe."

The news swept throughout the slave quarters of the southern plantations as soon as it was reported that England had recognized the Confederate States of America as separate and independent. Even as rumors of Lincoln's impending declaration of freedom for all slaves spread from town to town, black leaders secretly plotted their futures. To them it was clear that a triumphant Confederate army would now have a free hand to squash any attempt at a slave revolt. While individual black leaders from Texas to Virginia secretly debated their best course of action, many freedom seekers let their feet do their choosing; they fled in the night and followed the Drinking Gourd north along the Underground Railroad. Increasing numbers made their escape; many were caught and returned.

Late one December Sunday, after services at the African Zion Baptist Church of Wheylon Bridge, Georgia, the Reverend Zeke Carter met with five parishioners. The Rev. Carter was nervous but determined. His mission was dangerous.

"Ah want ay' all to know, Ah got word this mawn' that Atlanta an'Athens are ready. They's the last ones to join in, an' only this late cuz dey hadn't gottin' 'nuff weapons gathered. Don't know how's they did it but Joshua sez now they got a big collection of guns in dare han's. God help em."

"Amen, brother, Amen." responded the others in one low voice."

"God help us all," said Joshua Tobias with a solemn shake of his head. "Iffen we can take the arsenal like we hopes, we got a good chance."

"Amen, brother, Amen!"

Beulah Mae Brown was frightened. She was only seventeen, had seen a cousin and her father hanged for allegedly inciting a riot in town; she wanted nothing more than to escape the plantation where she filled cotton sacks from dawn till dusk. She saw her life as nothing but misery as far down the road as she could see, Lincoln's proclamation and her church leaders notwithstanding. Hadn't Rev. Ezekiel said that Lincoln's Freedom Decree didn't mean a thing to them unless they could escape to wherever the Yankee laws would protect them? Beulah Mae wanted desperately to believe that the Reverend Zeke could lead his followers to the "Promised Land," but she feared for the cost in blood that Freedom would charge them.

When the Church "services" broke up with the hymn "Crossin' Jordan", Beulah Mae walked quietly back to the cabins with the others. There were low words passed from head to head, but Beulah Mae heard them not.

"Beulah! Wa'sa matter wif you? Din't yah hear me?" It was "I.T," Beulah Mae's new boyfriend. Ismael Jefferson Thomas, I.T, had joined the Rev. Carter's congregation the month before when he mysteriously showed up among the cabins one night. He was an exceptionally handsome young man in Beulah Mae's eyes, though too

reckless she feared. I.T. had told her the long story of his flight to
freedom from a huge plantation in South Carolina. He had bragged
to her how he'd outwitted both Sheriff and hounds as he hid in the
swamps in daylight and floated by logs down rivers at night, ran
ridges through piney woods to the next swamp until he'd run into the
Rev. Carter's cabins on the Johnston Plantation two miles outside the
furthest edge of a little town called Montfort Junction. He'd eaten
nothing but snakes and catfish, and almost provided himself as dinner to a huge alligator two nights before he stopped at the plantation.
He'd been told by a neighboring field hand back from a coon hunt
that the Rev. Zeke had a safe house for runaways in Wheylon Bridge.

I.T. swore to Zeke that it was the smell of bacon that lured him to
take a chance on the Rev. Carter's cabin. "Otherwise I'd a kept goin'
all a' ways to Florida," insisted I.T.

"Now lissin' to me, Beulah Mae," said I.T. "I don't wancha to be
no feared fer me or the Reverend, or none of us. It's all gunna go like
I sez it is. Hell, if I kin run through swamps fer two, three hun'ert
miles in day or night, I reckin I can lead y' all safely down ta Florida,
what h'aint no more'n a week's sloggin through the Okefenokee.
Long as we got Toby Toms to guide us, I can provide the vittals.
Donchu worry yer head none, Beulah Mae. We's gunna make it.
Truss me, we kin do it."

Southern policy was not consistent from state to state. Border and
western fringes of the Confederacy did not share the same fear and
fervor of the deep southern areas like South Carolina and Alabama
where in some counties blacks outnumbered whites. There, it was
understood that slave holders were riding a tiger and holding onto its
tail for dear life. They dared not loosen their death grip for fear of
themselves being eaten alive.

Wherever white small landholders eked out a subsistence on their marginal farms, they shared none of the slave holding interests of the large plantation owners. Their only concern about whether or not the negroes gained freedom in their communities was whether or not they would become a cheap labor threat. As long as slavery was mainly the concern of the rich plantation owners, the free white farmers didn't consider it their problem. Even so, the least of them did not consider any black man their equal, or worthy of inclusion in their community. The lines of taboo were clearly and forever drawn in their minds. Let slave and slave owner coexist in whatever form they would, as long as it did not effect the small farmers' life; it was not their concern.

But it was a different matter in the heavily black areas of Virginia and South Carolina. Slave revolts had been put down with a heavy hand in the past and now new rumblings made the white communities uneasy. Militias were raised in every town. Black church gatherings were watched with growing suspicions. Northern abolitionist flyers appeared throughout the South. Tensions were dangerously rising like sparks flying in hot winds over fields and forests of dry tinder. Sheriff and slave holder targeted suspected black leaders as dangerous revolutionaries. They were arrested and held in jails without charge or trial.

For the large slave holders, the dilemma of riding the tiger posed an economic problem. Each slave represented an initial investment in money and as long as they worked the fields, they produced a return on that investment. No slave owner could afford to lose his investment either by rotting in jail as a potential rebel, or by escaping to freedom in the North. His best interests were served only by a productive field hand who could produce a constant income stream through labor compensated only by a subsistence amount of food, clothing and shelter. And so, in reality, slavery had divided the Confederate States of America into regions, counties, and states with varying degrees of dependence on the institution. In effect, the hard won principal of "State's Rights" when put to its ultimate economic test in the South, threatened to split state from state and regions of each state according to the overriding special interests of each community. In effect, the Confederacy was a loose bundling of individuals whose only real loyalty was to themselves; even though Virginians of every economic and social stratum had loudly proclaimed their allegiance to "their Country". They were all loyal to the Old Dominion and to Dixie, but united only by the belief that their real enemies were those "Damn Yankees."

Sooner or later, if left to their own devices, they would sort things out according to what each group and region felt was in their own best interest. Perhaps, as the Virginia delegates at the founding fathers' conventions had quietly insisted to Adams and Franklin, the slave states would never consent to a union with the non-slave states if the Northerners insisted on forcing their economic and moral principles on an unwilling South. Make war on slavery and there are no "United States". Respect each state to do its business as it will and a loose union may exist.

Now, with Lincoln's armed effort to force the North's principles on an unwilling South thwarted by an alliance of Richmond and London, Southern cotton and British textile mills were ready to enter an era of mutual prosperity. It was to be an unholy alliance, as many economic marriages so often prove to be. And if there was to be cheap labor to reap the cotton for the British textile machine, it surely would come from the usual source; Southern slave labor. The plantation system could not afford to allow any degree of freedom to its slaves, in spite of Mr. Lincoln's lofty proclamation.

The Presidential Guard
December 7, 1864

Beuford Forrest Ralston was beside himself with pride and joy; his captain had recommended him to duty in Richmond after Meade's surrender and England's recognition of the Confederacy effectively ended the War Between the States. Beuford's duty was no ordinary promotion, he was to serve on President Jefferson Davis's elite Presidential Guard.

When he reported to his new commanding officer, he had spiffed himself up in his new, tailored butternut gray uniform with a crimson belt sash. Beuford was so proud he could almost spit. If only his old mammy and pappy were here to see him sworn in. But his pa had died during the first year of the war, and his ma was down in the mouth and feeling poorly. Yet, with her son's upcoming pay raise she would not starve, as she had feared.

Captain Winston Thackeray Salem looked Beuford up and down, after he had read Corporal Ralston's letter of recommendation. In part it read: *"Mold this boy into a proper guardsman, I believe he will exceed your expectations in spite of his raw naivety. On the battlefield he proved himself to be either the bravest young man under General Lee's command or possibly the absolute dumbest jack-ass in the army. You decide." Signed, Captain William Sturtevant, 40th Virginia Infantry, Waynesboro Volunteers.*

"Well, Corporal Ralston, your captain had some interesting thoughts on your potential in the Guards. I see on your record you're a harness maker by trade. Does that mean you also have some experience handling mules?"

Beuford drew himself up tall, almost bringing his heels out of his boots. "Ah's driven many a cranky mule team back home in Waynesboro, suh. Why, Captain suh, if I do say so myself without 'pearin to braggin'--why there ain't a mule team born what I can't git to mind me. You might say mules is almost like kin to me."

"Hmmm. Well, we'll see. As soon as we got you settled into your indoctrination with the Presidential Guards I've got you in mind for a plum assignment that should test your mule skills." A faint smile crossed Captain Salem's military poker face as he answered Corporal Ralston's smart salute.

Two weeks later Beuford mopped the sweat off his steamy forehead. Even in mid-December in Richmond with two inches of snow outside the mule stables, the buildings were uncomfortably warm for Beuford's ten-man work detail. Shoveling three inches of manure off the stalls' floors worked up a sweat and an appetite for Beuford and his fellow mule tenders. They had been assured by Captain Salem that the surest way to ingratiate themselves to their four-footed charges was to groom them, feed them, exercise them and tend to their other needs; get to know both ends of the mule. It was the "other needs" that Beuford cursed with every shovelful. After all, he was not only a Corporal but a war hero. He should be directing privates to this task instead of performing the duties himself.

He was beginning to question his Captain's appreciation of his true mule skills when a month later he was summoned to Captain Winston Salem's office.

"Corporal Ralston, congratulations. I've received nothing but praise in your handling of your mule teams. It seems you are an artist at tending to both ends of your mules. I know you're wondering what happened to your responsibilities as guard duty to the president. Unfortunately, or fortunately, our unit has little to do these days after the war. Things are pretty quiet here in Richmond. However, that's not the case in all parts of the country. Matter of fact, things are looking damned ugly down around Atlanta, and especially in Macon county. There's been rumors of trouble brewing with the slaves on the big plantations. I've been ordered to send some elite units down there to beef up the Georgia militias. And you, Corporal Ralston, with your illustrious war record and your finely honed skills as a mule trainer, have been reassigned to that unit. Congratulations, Ralston. You leave in a fortnight. If you need time to go see your family before you depart we will allow you a week's leave."

Ralston slowly rendered a crisp salute while his befuddled mind tried to grasp the meaning of his new duty. He'd never been out of Northern Virginia, except for a brief excursion to Pennsylvania, or even set foot on one of the big, rich plantations he'd heard about. Trouble brewing in the great state of Georgia--- what did it all mean?

The Promised Land
March, 1865

Joshua Tobias leaned over I.T.'s shoulder in the dark March morning three hours before dawn. I.T. fiddled with the slim wire pick. He didn't need light, only stillness to feel and hear the inner mechanism of the heavy but crude padlock respond to his ticklings.

"It's comin', it's comin'," he whispered, as much to himself as to his co-felon. Breaking into a state arsenal was a felony in Georgia; but for a slave it would become a capital offense. Nevertheless, neither man hesitated to perform the dangerous mission their congregation had asked of them. Though they knew they could not use armed force in their flight to freedom in Florida, they needed the security of the threat of the gun barrel in any encounter with anyone who would oppose their escape from the plantation.

"Thunk," said the iron arm as the padlock unlocked its resistant mechanism. "Gotcha!" whispered a smiling Ishmael Jefferson Thomas. Joshua Tobias breathed out a long sigh of relief. Instead of taking as many rifles and pistols and ammo as the two could fill their burlap sacks with, they carefully selected six pistols and six rifles from the hundreds resting in their wooden racks. What they took would not be missed until someone did a complete inventory of the remainder and wondered why half a dozen of each were missing.

As I.T. carefully relocked the heavy padlock in place, the two conspirators silently stole back to their cabins where a fearfully anxious Rev. Carter awaited their return. In the darkness they carefully buried the contraband arms under the floorboards of three different cabins. Then they attempted a fitful sleep for the hour and a half left before the sun rose on the old Roman date marking the dawn of a new year, full of its promise of both hope and dread.

The date set for the escape of the 26 slaves of the Johnston Plantation on the outskirts of Wheylon Bridge, Georgia was flexible; they meant to depart around midnight of the first stormy night in May when thunderstorms would hide any sounds the little band might make to alarm anyone's hounds. I.T.'s plan was to make their way ten miles the first night, southeast to a tributary of the Suwannee River. He had scouted the route last November and found deer trails that skirted cabins and the scant habitations of the southern Georgia pine forest. Once on the tributary, the little band could drift quietly during the spring nights to the edge of the great swamp, the dismal Okefenokee, where with any luck they might encounter the remote bands of Seminoles still clinging to their ancestral homelands. Or they might continue the remaining fifty miles due south to freedom in northern Florida. Either way, only catfish and bullfrogs would be available to supplement their meagre and diminishing supply of dried foods carefully squirreled away in preparation for their long-anticipated flight to the Promised Land.

"Ah don't know rightly what happen to 'em," said the Rev. Ezekiel Carter with a sad look and shake of his gray head. "We ain't heard nuttin' from either Atlanta or Athens in three weeks. I fear for the worst. If our brothers was caught, we gotta pray that they weren't tortured to name us in the plan. Either way, we cain't delay no longer. First good thunderstorm, we gotta go. We can't wait no longer for a signal. It's all fer themselves now, I reckin. God help 'em."

"Amen." came the slow, low response from the five congregationalists gathered in Rev. Zeke's cabin. "Amen." They shuffled dejectedly, each back to his waiting family in the little cabins under the loblolly pines edging the Johnston Plantation's open cotton fields, where the hot, spring sun promised to heat up both cotton plants and slave tenders equally.

Mules--Richmond to Atlanta
April 24, 1865

The rumors flew among the detachment from the Jefferson Davis Presidential Guard recently assigned to duty in Atlanta. There were stories of recent slave revolts on several big cotton and rice plantations. It was said bands of negroes had broken into state militia arsenals in Macon, Athens and Atlanta and carried off huge quantities of arms and ammunitions. The band in Macon had been caught before they could do any damage and twenty-one slaves had been shot or hanged before they could rise up in revolt. Their leaders were tortured before being executed for treason against the state, but they had resisted till their last breath any information or name that could connect them to the other well-coordinated revolts.

"Jeeze, Beuford, I heard there was a couple hundred slaves what stole guns outta the arsenals in Athens and Atlanta. Imagine the massacres they woulda done if'n they coulda joined up and attacked the planters! Damn lucky someone saw them breakin' into the stores before they could do no real damage. Damn lucky the sheriff and the militias rounded 'em up and killed most of 'em. What a damned mess there woulda' been! What if we gotta do the same?"

Beuford was dead silent as he stroked his brush against the flank of his lead mule. It was only three weeks ago that he'd said good-bye to his ma in Waynesboro on the Shenandoah. His mind drifted back to the encounter he'd had with his childhood playmate and friend, Jeremiah Hunt.

"Beuford, you'll be careful, ya hear," Jeremiah had solemnly advised Beuford on the day he left Waynesboro. Jeremiah was not only one of Beuford's oldest friends, he had done his apprenticeship at Waylock's Harness Shop the same time as Beuford did. Jeremiah was an exacting and precise craftsman, greatly esteemed by old Mr. Waylock for his skills as a harness-maker. However, he was not so esteemed that he received equal pay to Beuford, even though they both turned out equal quantities of harness, if not equal in quality.

"You watch yerself, Beuford. I done heard them Georgia gals is mighty peachey and pritty. They'd love to latch onto a reliable harness man like you is. Don't yew fall for none of their tricks, we all wanchew to come back home, safe an' sound." He grinned a big toothsome smile, accented all the more by his mahogany complexion. "Doncha worry yerself none, Jerry. Ah ain't likely to pick me a

Georgia peach when my ole ma's got me lined up with some nice Shenandoah gals. Ain't none what bakes a sweet cherry pie like my Valley gals. Ahl' be back home 'fore you can shake a mule's tail in Feb'wary; you can count on that. An' dontchew let old man Waylock cheat you none on your work, even if'n he gives you room and board. You's worth a whole lot more'n you're gettin' if I do sez it myself."

Jeremiah looked skeptically at his old friend and playmate. He wondered that any white boy, even though they'd grown up together, played together, sat together at each other's dinner tables and now even worked together as free men; freedom recently bought by Jeremiah Hunt. He wondered if anyone who did not live the black life, swimming in a sea of white authority, could ever fully comprehend not only the daily life of a slave, but even of a freed slave. What would it take to comprehend the feel of walking in another's shoes? Still, he did not blame his friend for being who he was. Quite possibly if he, Jeremiah had grown up in Beuford Forrest Ralston's shoes he would see things exactly like Beuford did. And so they had parted as friends, happy for the times they had shared and genuinely hoping their separate ways would soon enough rejoin.

It was Jeremiah Hunt's parting smile that haunted Beuford when his mule-tending Presidential Guards mate retold the rumors of Atlanta and Athens slaves being rounded up for quick executions by rope and pistol for the treasonable act of violent revolt against their masters. In all his prior experiences of the horrors of war, with brother against brother, remembering the screams of dying horses and groaning men lying torn apart in the wheat and cornfields of Gettysburg, Chancellorsville, Antietam and the rest of the battlefields forever etched on his mind, the thought of his childhood friend Jeremiah Hunt kicking at the end of a rope, begging him to "Help me! Beuford ! Help me!" tore at his conscience like no other experience in his young life.

What would *he do* if his commanding officer ordered *him*, war hero Beuford Forrest Ralston to execute a rioting slave, desperate only to wrench himself free from his master's chains? What if he looked like Jeremiah? Beuford didn't answer his stable mate. He brushed his mule's flank more vigorously and cursed the "promotion" Captain Sturtevant had honored him with.

The Freedom Trail
May 5, 1865

The Rev. Ezekiel Carter looked out his cabin door as the evening clouds towered higher and higher over the western horizon.

"Lookey thar, marm. That looks like the storm we've been prayin' fer. Ah'll go alert the others to git ready. I think tonight's the night." He let out a long sigh of relief mixed with an apprehension he could not hide from his wife of forty years. Then he walked slowly from cabin to cabin and passed the word: "Holy Moses". Only I.T., Ishmael Jefferson Thomas, changed his expression from anxiety to a fierce determination.

"God help anyone who gits in my way for the next two weeks," he snarled. He reached under his pillow and pulled out his newly acquired pistol, waving it menacingly at an imaginary overseer.

"Ah'm beggin' yah, I.T. If you git hot under the collar and 'danger our escape plan you will surely git us all killed, man, woman an' chile. Remember you'se our true guide ta Florida; you is our Moses an' we need you alive--- an' don't chew forgit it!"

"Oh, don't yew worry none 'bout me, Rev'ren. Ah'm just sayin' ah'll die fightin' before they puts no more chains round my legs." I.T. spat on the floor for emphasis.

About midnight, the winds were whipping the new spring leaves off the tops of the oak trees behind the cabins. It was the wind before the storm, which promised a hurricane strength rain through the night. It promised both man and beast would seek shelter from the coming tempest; just what the band of slaves prayed for as the instrument of their deliverance.

Joshua Tobias could feel the throbbing in his right thumb. It had been his personal weather barometer for the fifteen years since the Johnston Plantation's overseer had cracked him on the hand with the walking stick he always waved threateningly whenever he perceived a slave to be slacking. Joshua's thumb had been broken and though it healed with only a chronically swollen joint, ever since then, it throbbed whenever a passing low pressure system presaged a storm.

"Lord, ah-mighty! It h'ain't throbbed so since that big hurricane last June!" He held up his alerted thumb for his wife and the four boys to see. He gazed lovingly at his family as they busily packed their gunny sacks with the two weeks' meager provisions they had been preparing for the months leading up to this night. Joshua looked around the little house he had lived in all his thirty-seven years. He would not lose a single nostalgic tear to be rid of the place.

The rain and lightning came shortly after midnight. By then the little band had followed single-file into the oak woods heavy with Spanish moss whipping through the wildly waving branches. Joshua Tobias and I.T. led the way south away from the Johnston Plantation and the village of Wheylon Bridge. Their first night's journey would take them south by southwest five miles to the junction of two small creeks that meandered in the lowlands through swamp and mangrove trees on its way to the big, wide, muddy Suwannee River. From there I.T. would be their guide, their Moses to The Promised Land.

"I know they're right 'round here, dammit! I hid 'em here myself just last week." I.T. was frustrated at not finding the six little boats he and Joshua had hid so carefully in the brush along the creek. He was answered by a tap on his shoulder.

"They's over here," whispered Joshua. "Only there ain't but five; one's missin'."

"Cain't be! Ah done hid 'em myself. Ain't no one coulda' foun' 'em in this brush. It musta drifted aways."

"Nevah you mind. We jist have ta bunch us up a bit more; we kin fit five or six to a boat."

The Rev. Carter sorted the little groups into the five flat bottomed boats-- one man at head and foot of each boat with three women and children in the middle. I.T. and Joshua were in the first and the last boats. I.T. and Joshua had carefully laid their plans; they wanted their six rifles and six pistols evenly divided among the men in six boats. Now they had only five boats, so I.T. armed himself with the extra pistol and gave the sixth rifle to Reverend Carter.

They quietly wedged themselves and their gunny sacks into the little rowboats and pushed off down the tiny creek to the accompaniment of peals of thunder with great flashes of lightning and heavy sheets of rain that slashed at them front and back. No one minded; the storm was their ally in the moment of escape to freedom and all but the children knew it.

Five flat bottomed rowboats, john boats actually, wove a slow winding course down an ever widening water path that snaked south by southeast through a mangrove swamp that Joshua knew in the dark like the route from his bedroom to the outhouse. He knew the current and how it pulled a john boat inevitably along its path toward the junction with the great, wide Suwannee River, ten hours or thirty miles away downstream, or as long as the storm lasted.

Joshua whispered low to Ezekiel Carter, "We's makin' good time Rev'run. Long about first light we'll pull into shore where we finds good cover and take our breakfast and hole up till dark. Can't risk bein' seen in daylight." The Reverend Carter nodded in agreement. This leg of the journey depended entirely on Joshua leading them safely down the Suwannee and into the great swamp of Okefenokee. Then it was up to I.T.

About five in the morning the sky was still dark and the ominous clouds still tumbled swiftly overhead, with only a slight hint of the winds shifting and diminishing. They had covered maybe half the distance to the Suwannee in five hours and the friendly darkness and rain promised that neither hound nor hunter would be out and about. As they passed by a thick stand of moss waving mangroves, Joshua halted his lead boat with his pole anchored in the mud. In the distance he could barely make out a low, gray form dead center of their water path. Was it some crazy fool out fishing for early morning catfish in this gale-force storm?

"Shhh... whispered Joshua, as he motioned the followers to pole their boats back behind the hanging mosses of the wide trunked mangroves. He was sure they had not been seen; fishermen always kept their attention fixed on their line and bobber if it was cats they were after.

"We'll just hafta' wait here till that fisherman decides to cut bait an' go home," Joshua whispered to the reverend. An hour passed and every time Joshua parted a clump of protective moss and peered around the massive mangrove trunk, the low, dark form was still there, dead in the channel blocking their route. But as a shaft of light from between the parting clouds rested on the "boat", Joshua let out a low groan of frustration. His "fishing boat" was a log caught against a short, man-sized stump. The way was clear, but now it was getting light and the rain had changed to a steady drizzle and the howl of the wind was now just a soft whistle in the leaves.

Joshua and the Reverend weighed their options and decided to move on as long as the clouds hid the sun and the rain continued to be their ally. Slowly, Joshua pushed his pole into the muddy bottom of the creek and motioned the others to follow. And so they continued on into a gray, wet morning. Then, emerging from the dark gloom of the mangrove swamp they came into a clearing with what looked like an abandoned cornfield that ran on a flat peninsula down to the creek.

The open field lay in the space of a hundred yards until it ended in a thick wall of pine forest. Before they covered half the distance to the pines, a rooster crowed. It was a greeting they did not embrace thankfully. Joshua motioned the paddlers to make more quickness, even as he and the reverend bent to their poles. Before the last john boat with I.T. manning the stern paddle reached the shelter of the dark wall of pines, the greeting they all dreaded echoed down the cornfield for all to hear. Some dirt farmer's old coonhound was baying a warning after their sniffed intrusion. As the lanky-legged brown hound bounded down to the edge of the water, I.T. thought quickly and reached into his bag of hound tricks. He leaned back and tossed a chunk of dried bacon towards the baying dog. It landed at the water's edge and in one swift lunge the coon hound snatched it and gulped it down seconds before his sibling hound arrived to dispute the gift that had unexpectedly answered his alarm call.

Minutes after the tiny fleet of almost-free slaves disappeared into the shadows of the welcoming pine forest lined creek, a yawning dirt farmer lunged at his hounds with a switch as they sniffed and lapped the water where once a lump of bacon had miraculously landed from heaven.

"Yew dumb jack-asses after muskrats agin'? Ain't I done tole yew to shut yer yaps when ah'm a sleepin'? Ah'll give ya whut fer!" And he swiped at the slower of the two sibling hounds as they bounded back up the cornfield to their shanty in the pines.

I.T. kept watch over his shoulder but now he could not even make out the dimly lit opening where the hounds had snatched his bacon. The combination of a heavy humidity and the cool temperature of the storm's atmosphere was brewing a thick fog swirling off the land and the water. Now he could barely see the boat ahead of him, let alone Joshua's lead boat. He gave the low whistle signal they had agreed on; the melodious notes of a Tennessee Warbler. Ahead in the mist came the equally melodious response. Then came the signal to halt and assemble; the hoot of the swamp loving barred owl. "Who-who-who-whoooo. Who-cooks-for-youuuuuu?"

Rising out of the soupy fog came first one, then two then three and four of the little fleet.

"The chillun' is hungry, wet and t'aaard," explained the Reverend Zeke. "We's safe in this fog so we think we can try to lite a fire with the pine needles and maybe we can dry out our clothes and eat sumpin', rest a little and then push off as long as this fog hides us. You might even catch us a catfish, I.T."

And so, twenty-six self-freed Johnston Plantation slaves huddled around a weak but welcome fire on the bank of the creek, almost to the Suwannee, tucked in the gloom of a dark, sheltering, pine grove.

Johnston Plantation, Georgia
May 6, 1865

Beuford had just finished feeding his mule team when he got word that the Captain wanted to see him. He kicked off his manure-caked boots and went straight to his bunk and pulled his uniform boots out from under the bed. He remembered what had happened the first time he walked directly from the mule barn to report to another urgent summons from the captain.

"Yes, suh! Captain!" Beuford gave Captain Winston Salem his usual crisp salute.

"At ease, Corporal. We just got orders to proceed down to a little town in southern Georgia where all the slaves from one plantation have run away. No great disaster, that, as far as we're concerned, 'cept for one thing; the local sheriff insists the county arsenal is missing guns and ammunition and he's afraid them escaped slaves are responsible. If so, that falls under my mission orders to aid in putting down any armed insurrections, preferably before they happen. So get your company of mule-tenders together, Corporal. Tomorrow morning we take the train to a little town name of Wheylon Bridge, Georgia.

Beuford cursed when the sergeant shook his bunk and bellowed at the snoozing mule-tenders. "Get movin' ya' lazy slugs or y'all don't git no breakfast!"

Just two days earlier, sun broken clouds had greeted Bentley Thetford Johnston as he stormed angrily from empty slave cabin to empty cabin. Fires smoldered in every one, giving early risers the impression their occupants were sleeping in late after the terrible storm that only now had simmered down to a foggy and intermittent, windy rain.

"Get the hounds!" he yelled at his overseer. They cain't 'a gone far in that storm!"

But the blue tick coonhounds found no scent, no trail, and they circled aimlessly and desperately sifted the air for any hint of a faint trail.

"Damnation, boss! It's too damn wet. Any scent them bastards woulda left is long gone washed away. Maybe I can find footprints in the mud; maybe in the oak woods. That's where they woulda gone."

"Well, get to it! Ah'm gunna go git the sheriff and his blood-hounds; they got better noses."

The better noses of the sheriff's hounds led from behind the cabins down a trail through the oak trees to the edge of a swamp that was fed by a little creek, a remote tributary that led to the big Suwannee River and south through the Great Okefenokee Swamp, then to the Florida line.

"That's where they're headed, ah'll bet mah Bible on it," thumped Bentley Johnston, smacking his fist into his open palm.

"Yer darn tootin' right on that account," echoed the sheriff. "Iffen I hada' make my escape plan, ah'd drift right down the cricks to the Big Suwannee and then high-tail it into the big swamp. Man could hide out there and never be found nor followed. By Jeezis, that's 'zackly whut ah'd do. Yessir!" He spat a gob of tobacco juice for emphasis.

The sheriff pondered the situation as he listened to the plantation lord and his overseer. He well appreciated the loss in capital and revenue the escaped slaves meant to the Johnston Plantation. But from years of hunting fugitive slaves he also understood the reality of the anticipated pursuit.

"I 'preciate yer loss, Bentley. But I want ya to know these things can end up badly if'n ya lose yer head and don't take things sensible and level-headed like. Now I want chew both ta calm down an' lissen ta me. Them slaves is gunna be tired, hungry, miserably wet and above all desperate to escape. These ain't no possums we be huntin'. Them's highly driven, thinkin' human bein's dead set ta gain their freedom, probably in Florida, an' mebbe further. And possibly armed."

"Yah Rexford, we'all know that!" spat the overseer, "but Florida ain't gunna do 'em no good. We got 'greements with the Florida people to hand escaped slaves right back ta us soon's they catch 'em. Won't do 'em a lick a good ta run ta Florida."

"Sure, an' that's all the more reason ta think this out mighty careful-like. We gotta head 'em off and outsmart 'em but if'n we go headstrong right at 'em guns a blazin' all yer gunna end up with, Bentley, is a pile 'a dead neegroes. An' thet ain't what yew want is it?"

"Awright, Rex, whadda ya propose we do?"

The next day as the sheriff read over his telegram from Atlanta, he dismissed his plan to raise a posse of locals, including Mr. Johnston and his overseer. He would gladly wait for the contingent of the Presidential Guard and Captain Winston Salem. He'd just as soon not try to lead a disgruntled slave-owner and his toady overseer with his omnipotent thrashing cane. Better to leave the responsibility for the eventual success, or failure, of this mission to the Confederate Army. Ultimately, the outcome of this or any other slave revolt or escape would depend on the political role President Jefferson Davis chose to play. Sheriff Rexford Daye was content to just do his duty in Wheylon Bridge and collect his paycheck as quietly as possible. He had no political or social axes to grind.

"Chrissakes, Beuford, what the 'ell are we doin' in this miserable little place?" said his fellow mule tender, Sinclair, as he looked up the main street of Wheylon Bridge.

"You heard the rumors same as Ah did," replied Corporal Ralston. "Someone's slaves done up and gone away. Cain't say as Ah blames 'em neither."

"Ah still don't see how our mules is gunna follow them folks down a river an' through the swamps. What are we s'pposed to help do?"

"They ain't gunna stay in the river, yew jack-ass. I heard the captain say we's gunna outflank 'em and catch 'em when they go ta dry land at the border. We's gunna race our wagon train straight dab down the Jacksonville Pike an' wait fer 'em somewheres near the edge a' that big ole swamp. Tha's what Ah heard, anyway."

Near the Florida Border
May 6, 1865

Corporal Beuford Ralston and his mule-team mate, Sinclair stood beside their supply wagons in the heavy morning fog.

"Jeezis, Beaford, ah cain't see the nose end of my mules from right by their rumps. How the 'ell's we s'posed ta see a bunch a darkies commin' down that trail?"

"If ya shut up we might hear 'em before's we see's 'em."

The little path that led from the banks of the Suwannee River was used by locals as an easy high ground trail around the mud flats this side of the Great Okefenokee Swamp. It was an old Seminole trail that afforded the best route south into the cypress woods surrounding the northern edge of the swamp. It was also known as the best place to hide out for remnant Seminole bands, fur-trapping hermits, outlaws and escaped slaves. A man or a small village could live off the creatures of the swamp and hide out forever and never be found.

"Ah don't know why that sheriff thinks they's gunna come by this trail, Sinclair. There must be a hundred ways they could get themselves into the cypress swamps and we'd never see hide nor tail of 'em."

"Well, Ah tells yew this is the way one of the farmers up-river said he saw a bunch of negroes in half a dozen boats, a high-tailin' it down the river. Says no sensible person could drag them boats over the mud flats. Says if'n they knows where they's goin' this is the trail they'd take."

Beuford, Sinclair and the baggage wagons were parked off to the side of an opening in the Seminole trail. Ahead, Captain Salem and the sheriff waited in ambush, hidden behind brush and the trunks of huge, old cypress trees. There they awaited for the little band of Johnston Plantation slaves. Captain Salem was relying on the judgment of a farmer who insisted their quarry would have to come down this trail within this day or the night or the next.

The Battle of Okefenokee
May 7, 1865

"Ishmael Jefferson Thomas! You is da stubbernist, damn man ah've evah known!" an exasperated Beulah Mae sputtered. "Here we's tryin' our best ta make a quiet an' peaceful move ta a new home in the Florida land and all's you got on yer mind is shootin' the first white sheriff what gits in yer way. An' lemme tell ya', I.T., you's gunna git yer wishes come true if'n yew keeps on a'fiddlin' with them pistols like yew do!"

"Lot yew know, Beulah! Lot yew know! What Ah do knows fer shure is soon's we cross paths with whoever's after us will be lookin' at yew an' me thru gun sights. Thas' fer damn shure. Jus' remember that!"

Beulah Mae thought about the sight of a posse of white men with hounds hot on their trail and shuddered. What would she do if I.T. shot at them instead of running? Her stomach wrenched and a wave of nausea swept up to her head and whirled in her ear drums. She realized the thumping in her ears was her heart sending a warning message upwards. Beulah Mae took a deep breath and slowly released the pent up air. She rested a comforting hand on her man's shoulder.

The Reverend Carter raised his hand to motion a halt. It had been only a half hour's slow walk down the pine needled narrow trail that Joshua said would lead by dry land into the northern edge of the great swamp where tangles of brush and vine provided an impenetrable cover in the midst of forests of loblolly pine and cypress trees. The fog that had sheltered their escape for two days was now evaporating and every shadowy tree trunk that loomed ahead on the wind-

85

ing trail appeared as some menacing apparition to the Reverend and his guide.

"Ah thought ah heard someone sneeze up yonder there," whispered Joshua to Reverend Carter. They stood dead still and listened. The only sound was a faint morning breeze whispering down to them from the uppermost branches of the loblolly pines. But it was the absence of bird voices that most alarmed Joshua. He waited and listened for the warning rasping of any alarmed crows ahead on the trail.

"There, Zeke, ya hear that! Them's crows alerting their fellows of intruders in their neighborhood."

"Better stay put," whispered the Reverend.

A hundred yards ahead, Sinclair expressed his growing impatience to his mule-mate. "How long are we 'sposed ta sit here?"

"Ya heard the captain, Sinclair. He thinks iffen they's movin' quick-like they'll show up this mornin'; iffen they's lolly-gaggin' it could be nighttime or even ta'morrah. So shut up an' eat yo' po'k chop."

Spread out on both sides of the trail were twenty armed guardsmen, hidden behind bushes as directed by Captain Salem. The sheriff said nothing about the Captain's idea of an ambush because he hadn't been consulted. Privately, he doubted the soldiers could stay quiet at their posts while being assaulted by heat, humidity and flocks of stinging and crawling insects, let alone the occasional rattlesnake. Just one badly-timed sneeze or cough would alert any wary traveller. And then there were the crows. They had kept up their alert caws ever since the little posse had set up their waiting ambush. The sheriff knew what that would signal to a knowledgeable woodsman, even if this smart, Virginia Captain didn't.

"Whadda we do now?" asked Reverend Carter. Joshua mulled over their options. There were no alternate side trails that he knew of, and since they had abandoned their boats, he realized they must either travel by night now, or bushwhack their own way off the trail. But that would be hard on the elders and the youngsters. Yet, they could not just stay where they were if there were people waiting for them somewhere down the path.

"We hafta hide till dark. And if there's dogs waitin' in the trail they'll find us soon's they're let loose. I think we gotta find our way around this trail."

I.T. had listened impatiently. Now he couldn't contain his impulsive urges any longer.

"We don' even know fer shure if thar's someone up yonder. An' fer all we know, it could be just some kids out pickin' skunk cabbage. Ah say, one of us should sneak up ahead an' see wha' s up. Ah ain't a'feared at what evah's up there."

"Even if you step in a hornet's nest I.T?" Joshua shook his head firmly. "Best if we's all togethah. You kin cover our rear if yew want. But Ah should lead the wimmin an' chilluns off aways inta the woods an' find a crick so's we kin fool the hounds, in case someone smart's after us with their dawgs."

"Let's git goin," whispered Reverend Carter. "Ah got a bad feelin' bout this situation."

I.T. sat up against the big pine trunk after the rest of the travelers had disappeared into the depths of the dark cypress and pine forest. Beulah Mae rested against his side. She would not desert her man, even though she mistrusted his basic instincts. She must stay his impulses with her steady common sense.

"Why dint ya go with 'em, Beulah? Ah don't need no help." I.T. said it defensively and Beulah Mae sensed that her man felt diminished by having a women share the important rear-guard position with him. It didn't matter that they were newlyweds and she had promised that she would stick with him, come what may. He scowled past her down the trail, now better lit with the passing of the morning's fog. He could make out each tree, bush and stump.

"Shhhh." he whispered, touching her shoulder. "Ah thought ah heard sumpin'."

Up above, the pine needles whispered softly. No other sound spoke to I.T. as he fingered his pistol. Then he heard it; a cough off in the distance. He guessed somewhere off to the right of the trail. How far, he couldn't judge. Then he heard a sound that sent a shiver up the back of his neck. A hound made a faint whine, and was stifled.

I.T. pulled the second pistol from his knapsack and motioned Beulah Mae towards the furthest pine tree. "Take cover behind that pine," he whispered. He peered around the broad trunk that shielded him from the trail. Fifty yards away he saw them coming. It was a short, thick man with two bloodhounds straining at their leash. One made a low whine, but quickly suppressed it when he felt the flick of the sheriff's lash pat his butt. Two men in uniform walked cautiously behind, both looking left and right as though counting heads at a county parade. The short man carried a shotgun in the crook of his left arm and both soldiers carried rifles at the ready.

I.T. knew he could not run and he knew the hounds already had his scent; that was why one whined. The breeze blew from the northwest and took Beulah Mae and I.T. directly to the hounds' noses. I.T. cursed himself for not thinking about scents and winds and hound noses. The short man knew what the hounds knew; men with a Johnston Plantation scent were somewhere ahead. He motioned the soldiers to halt. I.T. could not hear what they whispered, but he guessed. He thought they were arguing because the soldier pushed the short man aside and walked ahead with his uniformed mate while the short man stayed back and held his straining hounds in check. I.T. couldn't have know that the sheriff valued the lives of his expensive bloodhounds far above the glory and risk of capturing some desperate fugitives. He would let a reckless Presidential Guard Captain steal this glory. Let him have it, he wasn't about to risk his dogs in an ambush.

When he saw the hounds stop and the soldiers come ahead, for an instant I.T. thought they might not be detected, even though he was a mere ten yards off the path and Beulah Mae was twice that far in the woods. As the two soldiers came closer, I.T. crouched low behind the trunk. Looking over his shoulder he could not see Beulah. He shifted his weight and a twig snapped under his knee.

At the sound both soldiers snapped their rifles to their shoulders and stared in the direction of the warning. Impulsively, I.T. stuck his head just enough around the tree to see where the men were. The captain fired first, and a rifle bullet chipped the bark near I.T.'s head.

"Surrender, or you're dead!" shouted Captain Salem. There was no answer. Captain Salem motioned his lieutenant to circle ahead and around while he moved from tree to tree the opposite way. He had no way of knowing that there was only I.T. there and not twenty more men armed and squinting at the soldiers down rifle barrels. But, as the sheriff had already judged, this was a Captain eager for promotion and all risk be damned.

"Stop where yew are or we'll all start shootin'," bluffed I.T. The response came running down the path in the form of a swarm of uniformed riflemen, alerted at the Captain's first shot.

"Aw, Jessiz!" swore I.T. as he saw the running forms in dark gray coming to the aid of their Captain. He took a deep breath and felt the years of pent-up anger take over his senses. He raised both pistols and shot in the direction of the crouching Captain and was answered by a rifle off to his right. He aimed at the gray uniform plastered against the tree trunk a scant thirty yards away. His pistol shot was answered by a rifle bullet from Captain Salem that nicked his shoulder but hit no bone. I.T. winced and heard Beulah Mae crying behind her pine. In slow motion I.T. emptied his right hand pistol at the Captain, who once more offered, "Surrender or die!"

Before I.T. could answer, a hailstorm of lead cut through the low bushes around him as the company of riflemen fanned out and shot where Captain Salem directed their attention. Bullet after bullet tore into the shirt and pants of I.T. as he crawled behind his pine shield. He heard a wild scream and shouted to Beulah Mae to run.

"I.T! IT." she howled as she ran wildly, thoughtlessly not away from her new husband, but to the safety of his arms. A score of bullets buzzed and slashed at her as she stumbled towards the pine where her husband lay kicking and tearing the pine needled ground. She fell near his outstretched leg and pulled herself over his chest with her last gasping strength. Nothing but silence followed her final twitch. Even the crows were silent.

The captain held up his hand to his company and stared at the couple sprawled at the base of the giant pine.

"Oh, God! What a mess." He turned away and walked back down the path.

"Ah didn't know it was a woman," said a young, eighteen year old private to the group of rifle toters staring down at the result of their marksmanship. "Ah didn't know." His head slumped and he cried uncontrollably.

Through Briars and Brambles
Evening, May 7th

Joshua, Reverend Carter, and the rest of the band stopped in their tracks at the first gunshot. It echoed through the woods and told each one that I.T. was now in great danger. When they heard the responding flurry of gunfire, they all knew what was happening. Now they must make their run through the forest and the briars and the brambles and whatever sanctuary they could find. There was no use to make a stand and wait for a fight. What they had heard was evidence of a large hunting party on their trail. Next would come the sound they feared most; the baying of the hounds.

Captain Salem now ordered his mule teamsters to go and fetch the two dead fugitives and give them a proper burial on the site. Then he ordered Sheriff Rexford Daye to lead him into the woods and find the fugitives' trail with his bloodhounds.

"Now, jest a gosh-damn minute, Captain," drawled the sheriff. "The last thing yew wanna do is jump right onta their trail after alertin' them folks that we's close ta their heels. Whatta think they'll do efter they's heard all yer gunshots? Ah've seed too many times when's they's set up a ambush fer me as soon's they hears mah hounds efter them. Oh shure, Captain, yew'll catch 'em awright. An' yew'll shoot em all up. But they'll all be dead an so's half a yer men, too. Yew betcha; fer shure they will." He spat a gob of tobacco juice for emphasis.

Captain Salem reddened and he puffed himself up to his full height and glared down at the shorter, stout sheriff restraining his anxious hounds. "I'm in charge here and I'm ordering you ta'go find that trail! Now!"

"Orderin' me? Orderin? Ah ain't no goddam soldjer of yourn! An' Ah don't take no foolish orders, neither."

"You callin' me a fool?"

"Nawsir, Ah ain't callin' yew nothin' an' Ah ain't one myself. But ah'll tell yew what Ah am. Ah'm a man what's done this here job more'n once so Ah can tell yew man-to-man what's the best way ta' go about this here business."

Captain Salem calmed down a degree but stared malevolently down at the sheriff. He was not used to being disobeyed, let alone challenged, but he knew he couldn't afford to lose this man and his indispensable hounds. "Goddam civilians," he swore under his breath.

"Whazzat, Captain?" The sheriff gave a quizzical sideways look at the-red face above the high buttoned uniform, suffering in the late morning heat. Captain Salem turned abruptly on his heel and looked for someone in uniform to bully into submission. He bellowed at Beuford and his mule mates. "You two! Get a move on and go bury them fugitives and then get back here on the double."

Beuford and Sinclair stared down at the two very dead ex-slaves. They had both seen mangled bodies on many battlefields during five years of brutal warfare, but never had they witnessed a woman as victim. And a woman, any woman, black, white or in-between so obviously young was a shock to them both.

"God help her, Sinclair! Look how young she is. How could they have shot her down, so. She don't look no more'n fifteen or sixteen."

"Look there, Beuford. It's only him what's got a pistol; two of 'em. She warn't even armed."

"It ain't right," Beuford drawled out with a solemn shake of his head. "We never shot no woman when we fought for Massa' Robert. Nevah'; not black or mullatah. Nevah!"

"We ain't neither," answered Sinclair. "Gen'ral Beauregard woulda shot the man hisself what woulda done that to no woman. Fer damn shure, he woulda'. Make no matter what they was."

They buried the couple in a clearing among the loblolly pines and marked the spot with two crosses of tied up limbs. They told each other that for all the world it looked like the young woman had wanted to die with her man; that they might have been a black Romeo and his Juliette, dying together, rather than surrendering to the soldiers.

"Musta been, Sinclair. Otherwise she coulda run or surrender while he stood off the Captain an' his men." They nodded and shouldered their shovels and trudged solemnly back to the smoldering Captain.

In the meantime, Sheriff Daye had persuaded Captain Salem not to pursue his quarry till the next morning. If the ex-slaves indeed waited in ambush, let them wait till they chose to move again reasoned the sheriff. Then, with refreshed troops, supplies and a full day, pursue cautiously on the next dawn. He reasoned the fugitives were scared, hungry, and waiting somewhere down the trail. Or if panicked, were slogging through the mud and wearing themselves out in the heat of the day. Captain Salem could only sit and fume; he needed the sheriff's hounds and guidance and he found out the man would not be bullied.

Joshua held up his hand and motioned the band to halt. He pointed off to the right where several shadowy figures glided silently between patches of briar and brambles. "Reverend, tell the men to ready their rifles. We got company."

Before the Reverend could pass the word to the crouching band, a lone figure moved around the furthest bush and raised his right arm over his head. They could not make out his features but his form was short and sleek and it seemed to be a long-haired man in a flowing shirt carrying a rifle crooked in his left arm. He muttered something at them but they could not make out what he said. "Hokay. Hokay. Me hokay good." The seminole strode confidently up to Joshua, who crouched at the head of many dark, huddled figures. He looked them over carefully before motioning both to the right and the left. From hidden bushes and patches of tall swamp grass emerged ten bronze-faced men. All were armed with ancient muzzle-loading rifles, and some had long-shafted spears in their right hand, all adorned with colorful feathers and streamers, similar to the headgear they wore.

Joshua's first impression was that they moved like ghosts; smoothly, stealthily, silently. And that they were very colorful in their garb; not what he would expect for a band of hunters. He imagined they could just as well have been on parade, or dressed for a church social.

The shorter man who approached Joshua seemed to the Reverend Carter to be their leader. The Reverend now assumed his role as leader of his followers and stepped past Joshua to confront the Seminole, as they now assumed the strangers to be.

"We are runaway slaves from up north and we ask you for your guidance; for your help. Help us. Help."

The Seminole looked slowly around the fugitives and quickly understood the predicament the little band of dark people were in. He was not unfamiliar with runaway slaves; his clan of Northern Seminoles had rescued and hidden many such groups. Except that this bunch were more than the usual number and over half were young children and women. That would strain the resources of his own family group. Yet, no matter; the Florida Seminoles had sworn eternal war on the white settlers both of the ancestral homeland in Georgia as well as the newer interlopers across the border in the Florida territory. Understandably, they favored the enemies of the rebels, as well as fellow refugees from their common oppressors.

"We help you," he pronounced, looking stolidly into the black eyes with red halos that pleaded from the Reverend Ezekiel Carter's dirt-streaked face. "Come. Follow."

And so the Reverend Carter and the remaining two dozen now-free Johnston Plantation slaves retreated deep into the swamps of Northern Florida, guided into safety by earlier fugitives. The Seminoles themselves had fled the grasp of invading European settlers who earlier had coveted the ancestral homelands of the five "civilized tribes"--the Chickasaw, Creek, Cherokee, Choctaw, and Seminole.

The black fugitives would now find and make a new life for themselves; for now, free and independent in a remote region where the European settlers' civilization and Rule of Law could not touch them. They were now as free and wild as the creatures whose swamp they shared. Whatever bed they made for themselves was now their choice. They would live as their new Seminole neighbors did.

In the language of the Five Tribes, "Seminole" meant fugitives.

The Presidential Inquiry
May 11th, 1865

President Davis directed his cabinet's attention to his Secretary of War, Gen. Robert E. Lee. The secretary read aloud from the report received the prior afternoon.

*"Mr. Secretary, the Honorable General Robert E. Lee. It is my duty to inform you of our success on Monday, the 9th of May, 1865 in quelling a potential uprising of a group of plantation slaves recently escaped from their owner in the village of Wheylon Bridge, Georgia on the 5th of May, 1865. The armed insurgents, while attempting to make their escape to the Territory of Florida near the southern edge of the Great Okefenokee Swamp, laid ambush to a unit of the 40th Virginia Volunteers Honorary Presidential Guard, under the command of myself, Captain Winston Thackeray Salem. Only by noble and courageous action was my guard unit able to extricate itself from the dangerous situation and leave the field of battle unscathed with only the most minor of wounds inflicted by the band of insurgent slaves. Though pursued into the Great Okefenokee by hound and brave trooper, a number of the combatants managed to escape. We believe them to be but a handful who eluded our efforts to apprehend them, and though they have proven to be armed and dangerous, I intend to lead my courageous troops even into the heart of this vast quagmire until I am next able to report that we have extinguished this most dangerous flame of insurrection in our midst. The difficulties of pursuit in this most impenetrable of swamps can well be appreciated by any who know of its dangers imposed by catamounts, water moccasins, cottonmouths and rattlesnakes, as well as persistent bands of outlawed thieves, hermits, wild tribes of rogue Seminole Indians, escaped slaves and other such undesirables. I anticipate the transmission of a favorable conclusion to this episode when next I inform the Honorable Secretary of the War De-*partment of my success *in this endeavor.*

> *Respectfully submitted,*
> *Captain Winston Thackeray Salem,*
> *Commanding Officer, 40th Virginia Volunteers*
> *Presidential Guards (Signed) By his hand*

Jefferson Davis waved an impatient hand in the air as Gen. Lee put down the letter and laid his spectacles on the table.

"Robert, what the hell does that mean? Are the plantations in southern Georgia all up in arms or is this just one small isolated example like they turned out to be in Macon, Athens and Atlanta? He doesn't give me any numbers! Are we talking 10, 20 or a hundred slaves? What the hell's this idiot report supposed to tell us?"

Lee looked wearily at his Commander-in-Chief. His tired gray eyes had seen many reports like this for too many months. None turned out to be the start of another Nat Turner * Rebellion. In all cases they were wildly exaggerated or excited reports from every corner of the Confederacy that confirmed what everyone in the room knew to be the not unexpected truth: wherever the opportunity presented itself, desperate black Southerners would risk death in their efforts to gain their freedom in the North or anywhere else the Confederate Army or a sheriff's posse could not follow. Whether one-by-one following the Underground Railroad, or by a band of armed men leading the way to freedom, no slave anywhere could be trusted to serve his master except by force. Robert Lee had been weighing the implications of this truth for some time now since he had sworn his oath to protect the Nation as Secretary of the War Department.

"Mr. President, I doubt this is the seed of a Nat Turner rebellion. It's another incident in a long line of incidents that will inevitably follow as long as we adhere to this institution. We've gone over this before and we will continue to go down this road until we resolve to hammer out a means of achieving a balance between our needs and their wants. We all know the answer." He stared into the lined face of President Davis and locked eyes with him.

The president bridged his hands as if in prayer and rubbed his fingers up and down.

"Are you proposing we sit here today and as you say, hammer out our balancing plan? Do you think for one moment Stephens or any one in the Senate or House will agree to any proposal we make that effects their mighty "property rights"?

"I'm saying that we, each of us know what is best for the collective interests of the Confederacy in the long road ahead. We know in the short run we will be opposed, but it is a path we must put a foot on. It is our duty to lead the way as we know is best for all concerned."

"Dammit! Man! It's my head you're puttin' in the noose! You're their war hero; they won't blame you. I may as well hop off my horse and hand the reins to you, or someone else."

"It doesn't have to be that way, Sir. I will sign my name to any proclamation in as large letters as ever John Hancock laid to the Declaration. This will be just as important. It will lay the foundation for a new Confederacy that must work to succeed where our present state does not."

He folded his hands on the table and stared down his Commander in Chief and President of the Cabinet. He would not again falter in his mission to reform this union led by his beloved Old Dominion. Come what may.

* ***Nat Turner Rebellion*** - On August 21, 1831 an African-American slave in Southampton County, Virginia led a small group (50+) of armed slaves in revolt against their plantation masters. Nat Turner and an estimated 120 other blacks suspected of participating in the rebellion were caught and executed. The uprising resulted in the deaths of over 50 whites, and caused the enactment of new state laws that restricted previous rights of both slaves and free blacks.

PART TWO

An Inglorious Peace, an Elusive Dream

Boiling a Frog by Executive Order
June 12, 1865

"It is not enough to win a war;
it is more important to organize the peace." Aristotle

The President's Cabinet convened at 10 a.m. with the addition of the Speaker of the House and the President of the Senate. After a brief introduction of the sense of the cabinet as outlined by President Davis, the Speaker of the House stood to speak his private opinion and then the collective opinion of the House, as he saw it to be. As a Louisiana plantation owner he personally understood the difficulty of resolving the South's slavery issue with the least possible disruption to his own financial interests.

"Yes, Oliver Stantion, you may be seated when you address us. We don't stand on formality." Jeff Davis smiled at his clever play of words.

"Gennle'men, lemme tell y'all how we cooks a crawdad and a bullfrog in Bayou country. Fustess, they's but one way to cook a crawdad; fast and simple. Furst yah boils tha watah, then yah plunks 'im in, headfust. When he's done a minute laytah, he turns brite red and floats ta thah su'face. Tha's how we cooks ahr crawdads. But da bullfrog now, he's an altagethah diff'rent mattah. You dumps a live bullfrog headfust inta boilin'watah, he jumps back out, right quick like and likely scalds yah in da process. No, gennle'men, iffen yah'all aims ta cook that big ole bullfrog nice 'n tender so's he willingly slides contented like onta yoe plate, yah's gotta go 'bout it 'tirely different."

"Fer Chris' sake, Buttermilk, will yah git to the goddam point!" said an exasperated Pres. Davis, using the nickname Oliver Stantion gained from his habit of sucking on a jug of buttermilk during House debates. (He claimed it eased his gouty toe.)

"Now there, Jeff. Ah was just now gittin' ta the most important lesson for y'all ta consider. Ya don't jest throws yer bullfrog inta da boilin' watah! No Suuh! You let's 'em sit down all comfy like in nice luke warm water like they's used ta....then ev-ah so slowly, ya turns up da heat.Ya don't throw yer frogs inta the boilin' watah all at t'wunce. No, suh! By tha time they's done, they's boiled nice 'n ten-dah-- and all tha time they thought's they's on vacation! That's how we boils a spooky bull frog down in Lou'syanna." He folded his arms across his puffed out chest and set his lower lip in a superior, confidant posture.

"Yah, yah, yah, Oliver, I think we git yer drift. You're advocat-ing we take our slavery transformation policy one degree at a time, so slowly that folks falls asleep until we're all done cookin' the is-sue. Problem, is, Buttermilk, we may be talking a hell of a long time, and I don't know that we've got that much time! Anyone got their sumpin ta say? Whadda you say, Robert? You're the one that will take the brunt of all the attacks. You'n the army."

"Gentlemen, you know my home, my plantation and my work force is so close to our Northern border, I can smell Yankee bacon cooking in Washington breakfasts. I can smell the White House ci-gars when I step out my front door. So, yes I have given the issue much thought. It has always been a relatively easy journey for one of my dissatisfied servants and field hands to sneak across the border at night. It's an easy half hour for them, and yes, several of my best and most trusted servants have chosen to leave my service, even though they know I've always treated them with respect and fairness. But gentlemen, as we all know, when a man wants his freedom and can make that choice, whether he's black, white or mulatto, no chains on earth can hold him. That was true for my father in 1776 and it's true for even my most faithful stable groom a hundred years later. Freedom is a powerful potion."

"My personal policy has always been to treat my men and women as though they were a form of hired hand, which I believe they are. I try to explain to them that they are better off on my farm than most poor white farmers who struggle to support their families when crops fail, through drought, disease, pestilence and all the many trials that beset a farmer and his family. Most of them see the wisdom of what I say and appreciate their situation. A few do not. Nothing we say or can do will satisfy those folks. It is the majority we must appeal to. We must find a way that will convince them that together we can all work for our mutual benefit. That the freedom they are seeking often turns into a false promise. Without them staying on as my work force I will have to hire out poor white folks and pay them wages, while they will struggle to support their families.

I'm afraid the future for free black folks will turn out to be the freedom to compete with poor white folks for their old jobs. What I see for freed black families is a long, grim road of hardship. Will they see that? I don't know that they will. That, gentlemen is the answer only The Almighty knows."

Lee's monologue was met with silence all around the cabinet table. As he said so eloquently, only The Almighty had the answer. But Buttermilk Stantion couldn't resist a rebuttal.

"What yah say's mighty strong thought's Mr. Robert. Ah cain't say's Ah don't entirely agrees with yah. But you've avoided another issue that sticks in many a craw. An' that's about who gits the upper hand that long way's down tha road. Iffen we takes steps that gives the neegrahs some degree of freedom and sooner or later they outnumbahs us, what then, my friends? Do we just sit back and say,

"Well that's The Almighty's will? Ah knows folks that won't stand fer that. We'll have a bloodier war on our hands than this last one. Before we steps aside an' let's nature take her course, Ah'd like ta know what tha outcome'd be. An' believe you, me, it'd better be one that gives me tha favor or Ah'll nevah stand fer it-- no more'n my pore neegrahs gunna stand fer any one of us lordin' it over their futures. No suh, gennl'men, look a long ways down that road before ya'll make yer commitment. Look a mighty long ways." Oliver Buttermilk Stantion firmly set his jaw and rested his case.

Two weeks later, Resolution # 598 was signed by President Jefferson Davis and passed on to the House and Senate. The sense of the Presidential proposal was that every slave in the Confederacy was to earn his eventual freedom through a gradual process of steps that would lead from compensation for his labors, in exchange for a rental payment to his "employers" for food and housing expenses, to a time when he was free to terminate his employment and living arrangements and strike out on his own. The plan seemed workable but the devil lurked in its execution. Unaddressed was the issue of whose land would accommodate those "tenant farmers" who became freed. Where would they live? How would they survive? What would their status be in the community, once freed? It didn't matter, Resolution # 598 was vehemently opposed by nearly every member of the Confederate House and Senate. The country was not yet ready for even a gradual resolution of the institution of slavery.

The Waynesboro Volunteer Home Again

June 30, 1865

Beuford was greeted by his old pal and best friend, Jeb, his loyal beagle hound, now partially lame and rheumatic in his old dog's age. But the tail never stopped wagging, long after Beuford's old mother had cautiously opened the porch door to see her newly arrived son grinning down at her and scooping her up in his arms.

"Lan' sakes alive, son! Ah never 'speckted yew ta' git here so quick!" was all she kept repeating even after they sat down at the kitchen table.

"They let me go sooner's Ah thought, myself. Reckon they figured an old war hero like me deserved some consideration." He grinned at his ma and wrapped her shoulders up in his scrawny but wiry arms.

Beuford explained how Captain Salem had summoned him to his headquarters after they had returned to Atlanta. The captain had been angry and frustrated with the local sheriff for refusing to risk his hounds in the pursuit of the fugitive slaves, allowing them to escape. After a four day search of the swamp trails, both the sheriff and Captain Salem came to the same obvious conclusion; the ex-slaves of Johnston Plantation had indeed vanished into the Great Okefenokee Swamp with nary a trace.

Captain Salem told Corporal Ralston that the unit was ordered disbanded, its mission over. What he did not tell Beuford was that the Johnston Plantation owner had written his Congressman to complain of his loss and his opinion that the entire operation had been bungled by Captain Salem. So the unit was ordered to report back to Atlanta, disband and all members offered furlough while Captain

Winston Salem was re-assigned to duty behind a Richmond desk.

"What's that mean, son? What's a fur-low?" asked Mrs. Ralston of her grinning son finishing off another serving of grits and bacon grease.

"Ma, it means ah'm done with the army, at least the reg'lar one. They tole me Ah could go home now an' he'p with the harvest, and iffen ah wants ta' Ah can re-enlist in the ree-serves. 'Cept ah reckin the rumors was right; the army ain't got enuff money ta' pay soldiers ta' just sit around an' do nuthin' day efter day. That's the truth of the matter, Ah reckin. They jest cain't afford ta' pay me no more. So here Ah am!" He shoveled another fork full of grits and bacon into his grinning mouth as his proud mother beamed down at her returned prodigy.

The next morning, Beuford Forrest Ralston ambled down to the harness shop to talk employment with his old boss. Mr. Waylock was not as overjoyed to see him as Beuford expected.

"It's like this, Beuford. There's a heap of boys come back from the war. Seems all the Waynesboro Volunteers come back at once. Truth is, there ain't enuff work for all 'a ya. Fact is, Beuford, if I can use you back here in the harness shop, Ah'd hafta' let someone go. Now how can Ah do that in good conscience? How can Ah do that, Beuford?"

As Beuford left his old bosses' front office, he wandered back to the side yard to say "hey" to some of his old work-mates. One of the first to look up and recognize him was Jeremiah Hunt, his old boyhood friend and fellow apprentice harness-maker.

"Oh! My God! Is that yew Beuford?" smiled Jeremiah. "My how you's growed up now!"

"Yep. It's me. Done with the army now," said a dejected Beuford, shuffling his still shiny army boots in the red Virginia dirt.

"Yew comin' back ta' work, Beuford?"

"Naw. Ah's thinkin' Ah'd start a new trade. Maybe hire out as a teamster or sumpin'. Be ma own boss."

"Why tha's mighty fine, Beuford. You'd do right fine. Right fine." Jeremiah nodded his head approvingly and smiled at his old friend and work-mate's good fortune at turning his army experience into gainful employment.

The next day Beuford was summoned back to Waylock's Harness Shop.

"Ah got ta thinkin' Beuford, 'bout what a good worker you always was. Ah'd hate to lose you to one of my competitors. So Ah got to thinkin' 'bout what Ah said yestadee 'bout makin' room for you here. Iffen Ah let that negro, Jeremiah Hunt go, you could come back an' take his place. Ah know he's a good man, but you bein' a war-hero an' all; it just don't seem right Ah should keep him an' let you go. Whadda' ya' say, Beuford?"

Beuford didn't know what to say. He went home to wrangle it over in his mind, as he told Mr. Waylock. His first instinct was to jump at the revived opportunity; but his conscience leaned over and whispered in his ear: "T'wouldn't be right, Beuford. Jeremiah don't deserve to have you push him out the door."

Beuford rocked gently on the porch of his Shenandoah cabin, his corncob pipe wafting a lazy curl of tobacco smoke around his head like an angel's halo. The wisps of white smoke matched the prematurely gray wisps of sparse hair around his neighboring cousin's ears. Cousin Ralston Phineas Beauregard rocked next to Beuford, puffing in unison.

"Don't know rightly what ta tell ya, Beuford. Yer conscience kin tell ya one thing, but sooner or later yer empty pockets and yer empty stomach's gunna tell ya sumpin' 'tirely diff'rent."

"All I know's fer certain, is 'at lotsa folks come back from the war only ta find that their ole jobs is bin taken up by some or t'uther so-called "Freed Neegro". Be one thing iffen there was sumpin' fer alla us, but truth be told there ain't. So whatch gunna do? Let 'im keep yer ole job or take it back?"

"Neither ways, ah cain't win, Cuzzin. Won't feel good about it, neither ways. But like you says, Ah gotta eat just as much as Jeremiah do. An' Ah got ta think 'bout my ole marm, too. It's jest a damn bad sit'uashun alls 'round."

"Mebbe not, Beuford, mebbe not. Ah heard tell them Yankees in Washington has issued a proccle'mation what gives freed up neeg-gros a place to stay and sumpin' ta eats if they come live under them Yankees' protection."

"That so? That don't seem like the way ah heard it, Cuz."

"Wouldn't put nutt'n past them dumb-ass Yanks. Just remember, after Gen'ral McClellan bumped Lincoln outta the White House, all them freed slaves what couldn't find no work all moved into shacks all 'round the White House mansion. And begged the Yankees for hand-outs. Now them dumb-ass Yanks gotta support them 'scaped slaves what run up North; for their freedom they thought. An' every one of 'em is gunna supports whoever feeds 'em."

"Yaaah! Freedom. Freedom ta starve. Least on the Vir'ginny farms they all'as had sumpin' to eat. I knowd fer sure, Uncle Rex all'us treated his boys real good. Hell, they had food and shelter fer the little work he could squeeze outta them. Now what'll they get with their so-called freedom? Freedom to starve 'n beg, maybe."

"Wonder who them dumb-ass Yanks'll put in their White House next?" mused cousin Ralston.

"Dunno. Don't much care. They can put their Gen'ral Grant in charge or one of their 'mancipated neegros in their Lincoln bedroom for all I care." Beuford spat a gob of tobacco juice over the edge of the railing.

"Wouldn't that be sumpin'," laughed Ralston.

"But I doubt even their crooked politicians could pull that one over on their folks, even with all the freed colored folks they added to their votin' districts." Beuford spat out another gob.

"Them pore folks won't find no paradise up North," observed cousin Ralston." Fer one thing, it's too damn cold up there."

"Spose so," said Beuford thoughtfully. "Wonder what we'd do iffen we'as in their shoes?"

"Well we ain't in their shoes an' never will be. That's a fact. Ah knows what you or Ah'd do; we'd fight. Maybe we'd die, but we'd fight first. Jest like ya'll did with Gen'ral Lee. Hell if them darkies had sum gumption they woulda joined that rebellion down in Carolina and fought to make their own country. There fer shure woulda been enuff of 'em to make a good ole fight. Then maybe they coulda earned their freedom, fair 'n square, like you an' Marse Robert did."

"There might notta been 'nuff either white folks or blacks left standing if such a fight was to happen!" Beuford wiped his nose.

"Yeah, yer prob'ly right, Cuz. Yer prob'ly right. Trouble is, we ain't got it much better here 'an anywhere else in Dixie. Seems like ever since the Brits pushed the demand fer cotton higher, the big farms 'as been growin' a whole lot more cotton. Everybody's workin' now, and their slaves is needed more 'n ever, 'specially on them big farms. If they keep on growin' so much cotton and raisin' more 'n more slaves to fill the need, sooner or later we's gunna be up to our asses in colored folks. Then we'll be in the same boat's them Carolina folks. Then what, Beuford? Then what'll happen?"

"Damn'd if I know, Cuzzin. Damn'd if I know. It don't sound pritty. Don't sound like a pritty future a'tall. Least ways not fer us."

The Best Damn Cotton Picker in Ole Virginny
August 1865

Obediah Roach had tinkered with the idea of working at the local wagon shop. But something besides wood and wheels gnawed at his fertile mind. At age 22 he looked down the path of opportunity that loomed ahead of him. He a saw nothing but a grim, straight line that ended in a distant cemetery. It didn't interest him, whatever job security his employer promised. Obediah grew up on the edge of one of the big cotton plantations down on the York peninsula, and memories of watching the cotton harvest kept flooding his mind. And especially the job his pa had got him in the cotton mill shed. He'd spent hours in his early years helping the field hands feed the cotton mills and watch with a fascinated young mind as the teeth of Eli Whitney's magnificent invention did the work of pulling the seeds from the bolls; work that used to be done by young and elder slave girls. He often woke from dreams of listening to the hum and whir of Whitney's mill as it inexorably worked the mechanical magic that put so many scarred slave fingers out of work. Then one morning he awoke with a different dream.

Obediah sorted through his collection of odds and ends; wood boxes, slats, chain links, wire, nails and three old iron wheels. He saw the thing from his dream take shape in his mechanically fascinated mind. He labored over his contraption for two weeks. In the late evenings he wheeled it out into the nearest cotton field and tried it out. At first his wood and metal arms and fingers didn't quite chop the cotton stems as he envisioned. They made a mangled mess and jammed the collection box; the cotton plants fought back. But so did

Obediah. Small adjustments by little tinkerings created something that forced the cotton stalks to obey the will of Obediah Roach. Soon he had something that was absolutely obedient to Obediah. The damn thing worked!

Not only did Obediah's contraption work, it was designed and destined to free the slaves. They would be cotton-pickers no more. Obediah's Mechanical Cotton Picker, as his C.S.A. Patent was titled, would not only free the four million Southern slave laborers from the task that their masters had assigned them, it would inadvertently make them obsolete. The South, from that day forward would have less need of slave labor. Any menial tasks called for would be the job of the poor white folks and they would not welcome anyone willing or desperate to compete with them for the available jobs. Obediah Roach had indeed created a new Mechanical Cotton Picker and too soon it and its clones would replace the generations of black manual cotton pickers. Every big cotton plantation would soon acquire new shiny metal mechanical cotton reapers. Then there would be no need for slaves in the cotton fields. Then what?

Come What May
April 12, 1866

The President asked his secretary to schedule a break in his busy itinerary. "I'd like to see that play, *Our American Cousin*. Everyone in the capital's been raving about it I need a little comedy about now, and the missus can stand a smile and a laugh, too." Miss Jenkins booked their booth on the gallery of the popular theatre and assigned a newly recruited guardsman as the evening's security.

Halfway through the play, the young guardsman felt nature's call and hurried down the back steps and out the lower door to the darkened garden. He paid no attention to the black-cloaked gentleman approaching those same stairs, barely acknowledging his muffled "G'd eve'nin" in his urgent haste to water the tulips and return to his booth duty station.

As the guard bounded back up the stairs, the audience roared in applause at some jocularity onstage, punctuated by what sounded almost like two distant pistol shots. The reverberation of "imitation" gunfire sent a shiver up his spine in remembrance of Antietam and his decimated unit.

Then the crowd was crying out as if in a panic at some threat that only a fire could produce. In horror he reached the open door of the Presidential booth and saw Mrs. Davis cradling her husband's blood soaked head in her lap. She was crying and moaning and rocking back and forth all at once. The young guard heard the roar of an audience that may as well have been a crowd of Romans howling for blood in the Coliseum.

It was the head of Pres. Davis' Guardsman Jethro Pinkham II the newspapers were howling for the next morning. The darkly cloaked gentleman on the theater's staircase had played the role of assassin with no interference from Guardsman Pinkham. The fleeing assassin had broken his ankle jumping from the Presidential booth to the stage floor, which he missed. He landed in a heap in the brass section of the orchestra, where the entire trombone squad subdued him with their long metal instruments. He now lay unconscious in the Richmond Hospital, possibly in a coma from the head blows of the irate trombone players.

Since the reporters were unable to get a statement from him they turned their rabid focus on the delinquent Guardsman Pinkham II.

One month later, Private Jethro Pinkham II, stripped of rank but acquitted of any part in the plot by dint of his documented simplicity in all matters concerning thought processes, joined his superior officer, also demoted, in the furthest western outpost of Texas territory. The little fort, whose only purpose was to bait marauding Comanche bands into confronting the soldiers, provided an excuse for the commanding officer to pad his resume with reportedly gallant defensive actions against the savages.

The night President Davis died from an assassin's colt 44, the Secretary of the Defense Department issued a State of Emergency and assumed command as acting President of the Confederacy. The Vice President had also been wounded in the plot and was expected to eventually recover, though possibly as a spine injured cripple. Gen. Robert E. Lee ordered a thorough investigation into the assassin's background and the extent of the apparent conspiracy.

In the assassin's apartment were abolitionist pamphlets and a simple note that read:

"Sic Semper Tyrannus!"

In the November election that followed, General Robert E. Lee, Secretary of the Army & Defense Department of the Confederate States of America, was swept into the presidency in a landslide.

"The Drinkin' Gourd"
May 1, 1866

Jeremiah Hunt's loss of his job to Beuford stirred up Northern Virginia's abolitionists. Jeremiah brought his case to the local courts in pursuit of fairness in dealings with freed men such as he. The issue boiled over in local communities and then the Supreme Court in Richmond. West Virginia's abolitionists threatened to set up escape routes for all slaves seeking justice or freedom. The county was effectively divided; "half favored the abolitionists, half were for keeping the status quo, and the other half didn't give a damn!" So railed one newspaper.

Beuford Ralston felt it was all his fault. He was sure it was he who had caused Old Man Waylock to fire his boyhood friend and hire him in Jeremiah's stead. So Beuford felt duty bound with a huge side-order of guilt to take Jeremiah's side with the abolitionists.

While the courts deadlocked on the issue of dealing with freed black men in Northern Virginia, Beuford took another tack. He decided to run for local sheriff. He reasoned that he could somehow pay Jeremiah back by aiding other freed black men. What better position to help Jeremiah's cause than by getting into the office that could do the most good, or harm, on the local scene. Beuford knew that it was the Waynesboro Sheriff who most often was responsible for capturing and returning runaway slaves. He also was well aware that the sheriff could look with a blind eye anytime he chose.

He ran on the slogan "Vote for Your War Hero! Vote Beuford Ralston, Waynesboro Volunteers." To Beuford's mom's great surprise, her son won. Not by a landslide, but by a slim 33 votes. Even Jeremiah Hunt congratulated him.

"No hard feelings, Beuf. You deserve the job."

"Yep, an' now Ah won't have time for the harness shop no more, Jerry. You kin git yer ole job back!"

"Ah don't think so, Beuford. Old Man Waylock don't wanna look like his hand's being forced to hire me back. Don't matter. Made up my mind to go Nawth. Got a cousin that 'scaped Nawth to a little town in New Yawk. Village named Jamestown. Ever hear of it?"

"Can't rightly say's I have. But what'll you do there for work? They got a harness shop?"

"Cousin says there's lots a jobs in the furniture companies up there. That's what he does and I learned some carpentry trade before Waylock's when I was on the plantation. Pretty good cabinet maker if I do say so."

"Well, Ah'll be ding-danged if yew ain't the bee's biskits, Jerry! Ah sure hopes you kin do good fer yerself up Nawth. Ah sure hopes yew kin." Beuford smiled at his old friend and slapped him real friendly on the shoulder. Jeremiah looked patronizingly at the new sheriff, his one-time friend.

One week later, the childhood playmates parted company, each to travel totally different roads. The sheriff stayed in the comfort zone of his old community; the freed slave walked North along the valleys of the Blue Ridge and then the Alleghenies. He carefully travelled from safe house to safe house along the "Freedom Trail" of the underground railroad. Jeremiah Hunt was too cautious to trust the inhabitants of Northern Virginia, West Virginia and even southern Pennsylvania. Too many runaways were returned by bounty hunters, often sheriffs, who had Northern contacts. The bounty paid well and they were eager to sell out a passing slave, or even a freed slave. He knew he could trust his safe passage only to certain "railroaders" -- usually Quakers or Methodists.

One month later, Jeremiah breathed a deep sigh of relief. He had reached the house of Rev. Nathaniel and Bessie Quint on State Street in Pittsburg's East Side. He told them of his hope to find a new home with his cousin in the upriver town of Jamestown in the southwestern corner of New York State. The Quints had connections with one of the lumber rafters who drove logs from the villages around Jamestown. White pine logs were rafted down the Chadakoin and the Connewango to the Allegany River, then down to the junction of the Monongahela at Pittsburg. New furniture from the Jamestown factories recently began to make the same water journey by boat to Pittsburg, and beyond to the big cities downriver.

"Yes Jeremiah, we can certainly arrange safe passage for you back upriver with one of the furniture barges," promised the Rev. Quint.

So it happened that in the first week of September, 1866, Jeremiah Hunt, freed slave from Waynesboro, Virginia stepped off the barge onto the dock at the Chadakoin River's holding pond at the foot of First Street in bustling Jamestown, New York. He was full of hope and his mind echoed with the promises chanted by his Cousin Rexford Mason that this was indeed The Promised Land.

When he found his cousin he got a surprise. Rexford and five other freed-men were living in a boarding house on 7th Street in an area know locally as "Little Africa." It was run by a lively ex-slave of 50 years who had followed the Drinking Gourd when she was only 15. She was now a prosperous seamstress. Her name was Catherine Harris and her boarding house was a safe house on the Underground Railroad. "Miz Harris" as she was known, just happened to be a frequent correspondent with another ex-slave and strident abolitionist named Frederick Douglas, who had been on speaking terms with Abe Lincoln.

"You done landed yerself in Paradise!" gushed Cousin Rexford. "There's lottsa job op'rah-tunities fer yah here, Jerry!" He clapped his cousin on the shoulder for emphasis.

"Well, Rex, Ah gave this job thing lottsa thought whilst Ah's traveling, and I do believe Ah can hire out as a carpenter; seein's as yah say this place is full of furniture fact'ries."

"Oh, yah, they is. Lotssa furniture folks workin' here, Jerry. Ah'm sure you'll fit right in.

One of the lumbermen who had made a good start for himself after the war was a veteran who had been at Gettysburg when Beuford Ralston was there. But this veteran was on the losing side. His name was Alfred Werner Swanson. He'd been promoted to Corporal only three days before the Union Army's surrender on the Baltimore Pike.

Now, private citizen Swanson had parlayed his teen-age experience rafting pine logs down the rivers to Pittsburg and later to selecting hardwoods for a major furniture factory owned by a prominent citizen of Jamestown. The owner was a man named Reuben Fenton, and he was no ordinary citizen and businessman. While Private Swanson enlisted in the Union Army, Mr. Fenton was attending the Senate in Albany as Senator from his district in Chautauqua County. He balanced business and politics all through the war until 1866 when Senator Fenton was unexpectedly elected Governor. He had taken a liking to young Swanson and had elevated him to Assistant Manager of the furniture factory.

And so it was that early one bright October morning, Jeremiah Hunt found himself standing on a sawdust strewn factory floor discussing the fine points of doweling and rabbeting with a bright and sympathetic Assistant Manager of the Fenton Furniture Manufacturing Company. Jeremiah impressed Alfred. He got the job. He now truly felt like a free man.

Or so he thought. But there was something wrong in Paradise. There were only Miz Harris and seven other black females in the whole damned county. And every one of them was either too old for Jeremiah or as he declared to his cousin, "Too damn ugh-leee!"

It was a situation that held no promise for him. The other part of the female population he soon found out was off limits. He decided that this far North, the social climate was too chilly for his blood. It was time to retreat to the comparative comfort of his abolitionist

117

friends back in Pittsburgh, where there were many more young African ladies for him to choose from. Jeremiah followed the Drinking Gourd backwards on a southerly path to where the Allegany met the Monongahela.

The Sheriff of Wayne County
Summer, 1868

As Jeremiah explained to his old friend Beuford two years later when he returned to Waynesboro for his mother's funeral, up North he had felt like a stranger in a strange land. For Jeremiah the promise of The Promised Land rang hollow.

"It's a funny thing, Beuford. When Ah was in New Yawk, the churchy folk took me in and helped me find a job in a cabinet shop. Ah was a good worker, allus' has been. But no matter what, outside the good church folk, nobody took a warmin' to me. My cousin never mentioned that in his glowing reports. The people up Nawth acted like they'd nevah seen no black folk before; and Ah suspect many of 'em hadn't much. Ah'd walk down the street or go in the grocery store an' folks'd stare at me like Ah was some kinda' alien creature. What hurt the most was the little chillun. They's mammas would push 'em behind their skirts and give me a fake smile, but they'd try to shelter their little girls from me like Ah was some kinda' dangerous animal. Ah nevah got ovah that feeling of being unwanted. Feared actually. Rejected by them folks. That's why Ah 'ventually moved down river to Pittsburgh. They was almost no colored folks in New Yawk, but in Pittsburgh we had a nice big community. Of course, they separated us from THEIR neighborhoods, but at least we had a decent life together. Thas' where Ah met my wife, Lucinda. She's a dear creature, Beuford. You'd like her."

"Well, Ah'm shure glad yew got hitched and made a good life for yerselfs in Pittsburgh. But Ah don't doubt yew coulda' done purty good here, too,"

Jeremiah wrinkled his brow in deep furrows of exasperation and frustration. Beuford would never understand and no words or stories could throw light into his mind. He was Olde South through and through, albeit of a slightly more tolerant strain. There was no point in educating an old Blue Tick Hound to new ways of treeing possums. Still, Jeremiah couldn't resist pushing his one-time friend to the boundary limits.

"Now Beuford, do yew really think Ah could walk the streets here at night freely an' stop in the bar for a whisky with no fear for my neck? Ah can do that in Pittsburgh."

"You could, as long as Ah'm sheriff. And Ah'm *still* the sheriff. And in my neighborhood you'd be safe."

"An' if'n Ah walked down Main Street in broad daylight of a Sunday mawnin' on the way to church, and Ah tipped ma' hat to one of the purty little white girls; is ma' neck still safe Beuford?"

Beuford stared long and hard at the comment. He looked away past the barn down toward the river. A heavy evening fog rose over the water. It obscured the woods beyond. It was a fog he couldn't see through, but from past experience he knew what lay beyond. As to what lay beyond his friend's comment, Beuford could also see. But to Jeremiah's question, Beuford had no answer.

The very next day found Jeremiah and Beuford rowing down the river that meandered beyond the meadow and through the woods.It felt good to row his old clinker skiff down the Shenandoah to their favorite fishing hole. Beuford and Jeremiah hadn't been fishing together since the time Jeremiah had gone North. Now he was back to bury his old mother. It seemed natural to go fishing again with Beuford and remember the old times before the war.

"Good God, Beuford, I can't recollect when we'as last been gone to the ole fishin' hole. Before the war, tha's fer shure. Yessuh, jest before the Yanks come down here-ahs."

"Yep. Yew remember that big cat we landed?" added Beuford with a faraway look. "It was right on the edge of the big eddy. Took us a 'aff an hour to get 'im in the boat."

"Yessuh, it's all comin' back now. Yew remember them big pike teeth marks all across 'is back? Lan' sakes that musta been a mighty big pike judging by them marks."

"Yep. They's both was whoppahs. Mebbe we'll ketch their grandsons."

"Would'na that be sumpin'."

In those earlier days it would not have been proper for Beuford to be seen doing the rowing while a colored boy sat idle in the boat. Today, Beuford thought nothing of it. Back then, Jeremiah was a newly freed ex-slave who had worked and bought his freedom. He and Beuford had become work friends and a strong bond developed between them with a strength that surprised but frightened both. Now, here they were, years later, with wisps of gray tinging their temples, rowing down the Shenandoah to their favorite fishing spot. They talked easily of old times at the harness shop and exchanged stories of their separate paths since. Their paths had taken directly opposite directions; Beuford into local Waynesboro politics as a sheriff and Jeremiah up North to Western New York as a cabinet maker and later to a settled life in Pittsburgh in his old trade. Jeremiah had married and his wife had steered him onto a path of religion; he was a deacon in his AME Zion congregation.

"Golly, gee whiz, Jeremiah! Ah nevah pictured yew as a preacher. How'd that happen?"

"Oh, it was a long road, Beuford. Lot'sa little steps. Lost'sa little steps." He stuck his fishhook into a ball of chicken meal prepared that morning just before dawn, and plopped it overboard.

"Ah know's about them little steps, too. A mighty lot's changed in Waynesboro since the war ended. Mah times as sheriff showed me a whole heap about people hereabouts." He pierced a chicken dough ball with his hook and slid his line in behind the boat.

Jeremiah cast a skeptical sideways glance at his onetime friend. He knew in his heart that they now walked entirely different paths, one Northern, one still Olde South.

"How so's Waynesboro's changed?" He knew the answer, he just wanted to hear his old friend's new explanation.

"Well, fer one thing, Jerry, ah did mosta' the rowin' today. Nobody seein' us would question that now, but before the war, yew recall, it was all'as yew, the colored boy what haddta do the rowin'."

"And that signifies what?" Jeremiah suppressed a smirk.

"Well yew dang well know! Colored folks here abouts got it a whole lot better these days. They's plenty'a colored folks what own their own homes in town, fer 'zample. That's a big change right there."

"Yew might just as well say shacks, Beuford. I doubt they's not a single colored man what can afford a nice big house like the rich white folks up on the hill. No suh, Beuford, they ain't much that's changed round here."

"Well, what's it like up North then? Yew gunna git rich in Pittsburgh?"

"Ah'm trying, Beuford. Lord, Ah's tryin.' But we's still strangers in a strange land. In New Yawk Ah felt rejected by them folks. That's why Ah 'ventually moved back down river to Pittsburgh. Thas' why Ah got myself a Pittsburgh gal and joined up with her church."

"Well, Ah'm shure glad fer yah, Jerrry. Ah'm mighty glad fer yah both. But Ah still say things is gittin' better down here, even fer you colored folks."

"Nah, Beuford, like Ah says before, there's a heap a diff'rence tween folks down South an' them in Pittsburgh. Jest fer example, less' jest say Ah took a shine to one of them poor white gals down by the tracks. You really think ma neck'd be safe?"

"Aw, come on now, Jerry! You know better'n that! Ah'm sayin' we ALL's got our proper place. We know where we belong. Don't mean we can't all git along. Jest we gotta' be ourselves."

"Shure, shure. But what if a colored boy takes a likin' to a white gal. An' let's jest say she takes a shine to him. Then what happens, Beuford?"

"Aw! Come on, Jeremiah. Let's be fair. In the proper place we all can live together and keep our necks safe. But we's ALL got our *proper place*. Well, dang it all, even Ah cain't go givin' sportin' looks to no gal from up on the hill. Her pappy would just be doin' his duty to protect her for the proper gentlemen. Shoot, we all know that."

"OK, Beuford, but le'ss jest say...."

"Ah know where you're takin' me, Jeremiah, an' it ain't no good. You want to say it's all right fer a colored boy to take up with a white gal. Well, it's been done, and we all know what happens. Soon's you know it, all the chillun's turnin' out some kinda colored. But nevah do they turn out some kinda white. And that, Jeremiah is the nub of the matter. It plain ain't naturally fair. How'd *yew feel* if every time a colored boy an' a white gal mated the result was no trace of yer blood and all the chillun turned out lookin' white. Why in no time a'tall they wouldna' be *no more black folks* walkin' 'round. Every-body'd be *white folks* and yew an' yer kind'd be what them there sci-ence folks calls *ex-stinkt*. Then, what would ya' think a that?"

Jeremiah couldn't hold back a wry smile and a sideways look at his fishing buddy's flushed face. It was weather beaten and tanned from hat brim to collar, but the neck near the open shirt was a pink that never saw the sun of the day.

A tug on his line abruptly took his mind off the matter and shifted his concentration to the bend of his fishing pole. By the heft, he judged it to be a heavy catfish struggling mightily for its freedom.

The Glue That Binds
(Eight years later)

Beuford sat on his front porch with his cousin, Ralston P. Beau-regard. They rocked with a gentle Saturday morning breeze blowing the wisps of corncob pipe smoke down toward the meadow.

"Did ya see the newspaper this week, Rallie?" Beuford slapped his knee with the folded up paper.

"Yup. Shure did. And ah know 'zactly what yer gunna tell me, Cuzzin." He gave Beuford a knowing sideways glance. "Ah knew them pollytishuns up in Richmond would nevvah come to any solu-tion that'd benefit you an' me Beuford."

"Ah reckon that's the truth of it Rallie. But yah know, it's been that way from the first day we blasted Fort Sumper back in '61. The pollytishuns and the gen'rals all said we'd beat the heck outta them Yanks and it'd all be ovah in two weeks, and everyone would pros-per and be happy."

"Shure, an' Ah believed em. Yew did too, dincha?"

"Yup, they says we'as fightin' fer "States Rights." That was their rallying cry, and they promised we'd be better off without them Yankee pollytishuns tellin' us all what was best fer us. Yup, that was the idea. That was why Ah joined up and got to fight them Yanks with Gen'ral Lee. God bless 'im."

"Well Ah'm sorry they didn't let me join up 'cause a my bad knee. Ah coulda at least rid a horse. Yew know Ah coulda, Beuford."

"Yah, an' tha's another thing Rallie. Remember all that talk 'bout how them Yanks weren't no damn good as calvary? Remember how ole Jeb Stuart was supposed ta ride plumb thru them Yankee horsemen? Lemme tell yah, Ah saw some of them calvary battles, an' Ah kin tell yah, there was some damn smart boys in blue givin' ole Jeb what fer! Ah'll give 'em that. Yessir, ah'll give 'em credit there. Anyhow, back to that there article in the newspaper about President Lee's latest plan with the big slave owners. Whaddya think 'bout that one, Rallie?"

"Jeezus, Cuzzin! Ah don't rightly know no more. Just 'cause President Lee says he aims to free all his slaves when he dies, an' then tell his 'airs ta pay 'em wages ta do their old jobs, somehow that's supposed to benefit you an' me? Now, how the hell's that gunna do me an' you no good? Ah axe yew, Beuford, how do Ah come outta that if everybody makes all the slaves free an' then hires 'em back an' pays 'em ta do their ole work? How's that gunna help me?"

"Well now, Ah knows from facts right here in Waynesboro what happens when freed neegroes get to fight pore white farmers for the few jobs what's available. Soons yew know it, the neegroes was offerin' ta do the work fer less money than the white boys . Ah knows farmers what couldna compete in some cases. They ended up as tenants to the bigger farmers; they lost their land. Shucks Rallie, they might's just as well be a freed black man themselves since they had ta hire out to the big farms an' work like the colored folks, too."

"Damn right, Beuford! That's 'zactly what Ah sees happenin! Thas it eggs-zactly! Yew gunna end up with a whole county full a black boys out-competin' our pore white boys. Thas just what it's gunna end up as. You mark my words! Cuz! Yew mark my words!"

"Well, 'cording ta this here article from Richmond, Gen'ral Lee was just suggestin' that the big plantations foller his lead with their slaves. He says here that iffen they don't act soon, we're lookin' at another civilian war, he says--a bloody war from Texas ta Tennessee when black folks finally outnumber us an' take it inta their heads ta fight fer their freedom. He's warnin' the big boys to settle up now."

"Aw, Beuford! Yew don't think fer one minute them big rich plantation boys are evah gunna give up what they calls their property rights without a fight? Hell, like Ah sez many a time, they got a tiger by the tail and they know's it. There ain't no way they's gunna let go. But, Ah agree with President Lee, that iffen all them slaves evah gits their hands on enuff guns, they's gunna be Hell ta pay! Damn right, Cuzzin', they's gunna be Hell ta pay from one end a Dixie ta 'tuther. Hell ta bloody Hell!"

Beuford scratched his left ear with his free hand. He rekindled his pipe and drew a long, slow draft. He was thinking.

"Yah know, Rallie, neither yew nor me evah owned us no slave. Heck we couldna afford one iffen we aimed ta. But Ah think about my ole pal, Jeremiah Hunt, a free man now up in Pittsburgh. If Jerry stayed down here and Ah haddta fight 'im fer a job on some rich guy's farm, Ah shure hopes we'd nevah come ta the point a killin' each other. Ah saw what war was like, close up and real personal. Ah saw one a mah best friend's head git blowed clean off. It'll be bad all 'round iffen there's evah a real fightin' battle twix us an' them. An' all fer the sake a who gits the jobs; nevah mind 'bout who's free or not."

"That ain't but the half of it, Beuford. The part about the President's article what really caught mah eye was that thing about raisin' taxes ta pay fer their grand plan. Ah don't own no damn slaves and Ah'll be damned iffen Ah'll pay ta help the big boys sort out their problems. Hell, they brought those troubles down on themselves. They nevah axed me my opinion about how ta pick their damn cotton. Not that Ah would. That's their neegroes' jobs. But, alls Ah'm sayin' is it ain't mah problem what happens in the big Virginny plantashuns, an' it ain't mah problem what happens in Texas, or Joe'jah, or any uthah place in the country. It ain't mah problem and Ah ain't gunna fix them pollytishuns' problems by payin their taxes! Nevah!"

Beuford looked over at his cousin, now very red in the face for all the steam he let out. "Yah know, Rallie, it ain't jest the little guy like you an' me what's upset with the way the country's being run. It's the big folks, too; in all the states. Ah think even the guv'ners are afraid of the control an' the power that might come outta Richmond. Ah remember when the war started they was a Guv'ner, Ah think from Texas, what said we was headin' down the wrong path to break away an' fight against Abe Lincoln. He said the Yankees warn't the real problem. He said the problem was we was too dependent on a system that run on just cotton an' tobaccy. Cain't remember his name. He was hero of their Independence, an' he warned that we must put our own house in order first. Ah don't know rightly jest what he meant, but his own folks turned against 'im. Ah don't claim ta understand such things but maybe he was right about cleaning up the mess in our own house."

"Ah don't know neither, Beuford. Ah don't know what the answer is. But yer right. We jest may be headin' towards a real big bloody war with the black folks. Specially where we's outnumbered. Shure's hell glad we don't live in South Caralina or Joe'jah."

"Or Mississippi or Allybamy neither! Like yah says, Ah cain't see as them boys in Richmond got any solutions that is gunna benefit you an' me. Fer shure, alls they think 'bout is how to feather their own nests. You an' me Rallie, we ain't of no account ta them. Nevah will be, exceptin' when they needs some un ta fight their battles fer them. Then they'll wanna come lookin' fer us ta help 'em out."

"Now, Beuford, don't that sound just like 1861 all ovah again?"

While Beuford and his cousin discussed the bits of wisdom revealed to them in the latest news out of the capital, a disillusioned President Robert E. Lee pondered the fate of his country. Unlike his duty as head of the Army of Northern Virginia, as President of the Confederate States of America, he was only a figurehead with little power. He ruled over eleven states who fought central authority at every turn. It was a battle President Lee could not win. The civilians at his command were in it "every man for himself." They did not follow the President as they had followed the General

The glue that early on had bound the states of the Confederacy was now coming unstuck. It was coming un-glued in all the little farms, towns and villages where the big manor houses and plantations had never taken root. It was coming un-glued among all the discontented small folk who now realized that life under the new confederacy was no better than they'd had it when they were all together in the original United States. For them, the issue of slavery, its preservation or abolition had no meaning in their lives. A decent job and a decent living were all that really mattered and the rumors of the bustling prosperity north of the Mason-Dixon line was beginning to cause some to question the wisdom of their leaders.

Now a new call resounded into the Confederate States. As the old Northwest territories had become new states in the Union, the Dakota territory followed Wisconsin, Minnesota and Iowa into Northern statehood. Northern politicians had created a far-sighted plan to relieve the growing burden of refugee immigrants flooding their inner cities. A wave of ex-slaves clashed with a tidal wave of European immigrants, especially the Irish laborers. New York City riots erupted with Irish and Blacks competing for unskilled jobs. In response, the politicians created The Homestead Act. The plan was to clear the Western Plains of troublesome Native American tribes and fill the wide open spaces with landless Yankees, together with the new European arrivals and the Africans streaming in from the South. All who could wield a mule and a plow to improve 160 acres on Indian lands would be granted title to the property. The plan was to develop the fertile land of the western prairies, beginning with Kansas and Nebraska, into a breadbasket that would feed the teeming masses back East. However, any rebel from the recent war need not apply.

But the politicians did not mind if some of the land takers were one-time slaves from Dixie. Anyone on speaking terms with a plow and a team of horses would do. Now the only task was to remove the original landowners, the Sioux, Cheyenne, Osage, Arapahoe, Crow, Kiowa, Pawnee and the other native Americans living between the Mississippi and the Rockies.

The Morning Star
June 24, 1876
"In war, Truth is the first casualty."   Aeschylus

He sat his horse easily, like a chevalier long accustomed to the military saddle. It was a hot midsummer evening and the breeze blowing atop the ridge that looked down into the valley barely ruffled his blond, shoulder length hair. His red silk neckerchief set off the fringed buckskin jacket and the black broad-brimmed campaign hat. A long plume stuck in his hatband completed the flamboyant costume of the West Point graduate who had finished 346th in the 1859 class of 346.

His Crow scouts had pointed out the encampment of Lakota and Cheyenne buffalo hunters, who had pitched their tipis along a river in the Montana foothills they called the "Greasy Grass." On the military maps it was labeled "Little Big Horn."

The Crows alerted the horse chieftain to the positions of 10,000 enemy tribesmen. Men, women and children all spread out over several miles along their Greasy Grass river. The soldier with the long blond hair, wide-brimmed hat and buckskin fringed jacket scoffed at the Crow scouts' preposterous exaggeration.

"We attack at dawn. I'll show them renegades that their "Morning Star" will wake 'em up like the noon-day sun! They'll find out the Seventh Cavalry will ride through the whole damn Sioux nation like a hot knife through butter!"

The Crow scouts looked at him and held their tongues. They knew his reputation; his Civil War record as a daring, impetuous leader. They called him "Yellow Hair". The seven confederated tribes of the Lakota called him "The Morning Star". His jealous military rivals back in Washington called him "that ambitious, arrogant bastard." His political allies called him their best hope for the upcoming presidential election. All he needed was a headline grabbing military victory against the troublesome native Americans out West. The stubborn tribes in Montana had refused to give up their lands and their freedom without a fight.

No doubt the natives the Eastern news reporters called the

"Sioux" would have liked to hang the Morning Star's long golden curls from their coup stick. He had been part of Gen. Miles' western army of the Northern Union States that drove the Lakota from their sacred Black Hills. He was on their scalp list ever since. For his part, in his build-up to a bid for the presidency, he had told the Eastern press, "Give me 500 cavalrymen and I will ride through the whole Sioux nation." His ego was even greater than his civil war reputation implied.

In the early morning air of June 25, bugles of the 7th cavalry blared the charge and three units of the 7th galloped toward the encampment from three directions. From one of the tipis near the center of the Lakota campgrounds, Gall's wife prodded the embers of her cooking fire with a long willow branch. She was up at dawn to prepare her war-chief husband's breakfast. She looked over the eastern ridge above the Greasy Grass to admire the morning star twinkling brightly down on the many thousand tipis of the Lakota and their cousins the Northern Cheyenne, plus a scattering of Arapaho, down from their land near the Blackfeet. At the blare of the first bugle notes she turned to the North and stared at the improbable sight of blue horsemen galloping furiously along the stream bed towards her. She dropped her stick and ran towards the tipi, screaming the alarm as rifle and pistol shots exploded. Two of her daughters, little two year old Red Bird and five year old Pear Blossom ran from the open flap of the tipi towards their mother.

"Go back! Go back Blossom!" she screamed at her panicked little daughters, as she wrapped her blanket protectively around them and tugged them to the tipi.

The first cavalrymen in the double line broke towards the frightened mother and daughters and fired their pistols into the blanket shielded bundle in front of Gall's tipi. They galloped on and indiscriminately shot down anyone within pistol or rifle range, man woman, or child.

Among the first to die in the Hunkpapa Lakota camp was Chief Gall's wife and two children. Gall himself burst from his lodge, rifle in hand and fired after the racing line of blue clad soldiers. Oglala men, with rifles, pistols, bows and arrows now erupted from their tipis like a swarm of hornets, firing after the horsemen galloping along the edge of the river. Gall shouted out orders to his yelling tribesmen, as a second series of bugle notes sounded from the ridge above the Greasy Grass. He pointed his rifle towards the threat from the new warning.

"Black Cloud! Stay here with many men! Defend the village! Everyone else grab your ponies and follow me. We must stop them before they come down off the ridge!" They ran to the pony herd at the center of their circle of tipis and mounting, raced up the river towards a ravine they knew led to the heights above the village. As Gall's mounted warriors reached the plain at the top of the ridge, he saw Crazy Horse was already leading a huge force of Oglala and Cheyenne warriors over a rise that obscured a tell-tale plume of sun-streaked dust from many horsemen. Topping the ridge, Gall saw a melee of men, some mounted, some running, swirling and yelling amid the battle din of exploding pistol and rifle fire.

Crazy Horse, war chief of the Oglala Sioux, urged his men into the battle; "It's a good day to die, my brothers! Follow me and wipe them all out!" he shouted.

Most of the blue jacketed riders were already on the ground, dead or dying or begging. Gall saw several soldiers racing away from the main swirl in a panicked attempt to escape the slaughter. He rode one down and clubbed him out of his saddle with one swipe of his rifle. He killed him with his pistol. Looking all around, Gall saw no more fleeing riders. All were dead or being silenced by knife or gunshot as they crawled on the ground. Many enemy spirits were taken by the enraged native Montanans as they took the hair off the tops of heads (so as to claim the enemy's spirit in the afterworld) or stabbed or cut off offending parts such as an enemy hand so as to render them useless as future enemies in the spirit world.

Before the sun rose enough to illuminate the battlefield, all 234 horsemen of The Morning Star's unit of the 7th Cavalry lay dead, including the rider known to Gall as Yellow Hair.

Crazy Horse galloped around the fallen star. "Do not touch the Yellow Hair's scalp! We know his head was touched by the Great Spirit. That is why he led this small group of warriors against the entire strength of the Lakota and our Cheyenne and Arapaho allies He was a mad man! We leave him for the buzzards and the ravens and Brother Coyote and the Great Spirit! We have done well, my brothers; now let us go and give thanks for our great victory!"

According to Eastern newspapers that reported the battle, a heroic Lt. Colonel George Armstrong Custer had been ambushed, overwhelmed and eventually massacred by a horde of hostile Indians after putting up a gallant stand against thousands of the savages.

In the Lakota encampments, Gall told the story after the battle sounds stopped. "We wiped out Yellow Hair's men in the time it takes to eat our breakfast. The blue men ran in all directions like scared rabbits, some throwing down their guns and begging for mercy. We killed them all quickly." But for Chief Gall, at the end of the day, victory had claimed a high price: two of his wives, two daughters and one of his sons lay dead by his tipi.

Gall, Crazy Horse and Tatanka Yotanka, the Sitting Bull, had won the Battle of the Greasy Grass. They had wiped out over 250 of Custer's men. They had battered Benteen's boys. They had bloodied the nose of the arrogant 7th Cavalry. Yes, the Lakota had won the

Battle of the Greasy Grass. But the war had just begun. The Union Army of the West soon brought all its formidable cannon, machine guns, repeating rifles and an overwhelming supply of ammunition against the Seven tribes of the Lakota and their Cheyenne and Arapaho allies.

The Native Americans were driven off their ancestral lands and the survivors were herded onto scraps of wasteland where they were in effect contained by martial law in what amounted to an early form of concentration camp. The same government that had fought its southern neighbors and cousins in part to "save the Union" and in part under the banner of a moral cause "to abolish slavery" now set out to effectively enslave or eliminate the Native Americans. The goal of the invaders was to secure the tribal lands as the culmination of a policy of "Manifest Destiny."

While the western lands were being cleared, a growing stream of Africans left the Confederate States of America by whatever means they could and sought jobs and land in the North. They thought they would find freedom under the protection of the United States of the North. Hadn't the abolitionists trumpeted the rule of law and principles of justice for all; as proclaimed in the Constitution 100 years earlier by an eloquent Virginia slaveholder?

What the freed African slaves found in the Northern states was booming industry poised to change a farming society into a city/ factory society. While the slaves streamed North, another steady stream of Northern European refugees from poverty flowed into the newly opened prairies and plains as they became cleared of their native populations. The Homestead Act offered Europeans "free" land on the condition of turning it into a productive breadbasket to feed the eastern factory workers of the booming industrial machine.

Later, Africans too, were offered a plot of Indian land. Most stayed in the industrial cities. They were free now; free to compete for wages, free to fight for a new status in the northern "pecking order." They were free, free to join the universal struggle for survival in an unfamiliar fast-paced "Yankee" culture. They had found a new land, a new opportunity. They had followed a new moon, a Yankee Moon, that rose near the Drinking Gourd.

Independence Day-Southern Style
July 4, 1876

The morning of July 4, 1876 dawned with a fiery red-orange blaze spreading from horizon to horizon over the Wilberton Plantation outside Decatur, Georgia. By 7:00 am the temperature and humidity had both reached the lower 80s. The field hands had already been in the cotton fields two hours, and some had already felt the whip of Horatio Doolitttle. The plantation's overseer was a powerfully built man of 40 and possessed of a nasty disposition. He hated his job, but not because of the demands of driving the plantation's 120 slaves in the fields.

What Horatio resented was the requirement of being out in the hot fields himself, under a constant blazing sun and charged with enforcing the work demands of his own master.

"Move along there, Moe, ya lazy bastard!" He gave the slow-moving elder slave a crack of the bullwhip, dangerously near old Moe's right ear. The overseer was sweating as much as his driven charges, though his job placed no demands on hands and lower back.

Off to old Moe's left, and partially hidden from the overseer's line of sight, a younger, fit black man scratched the black dirt beneath the cotton plants with a hoe. He glanced furtively at Moe and the hovering overseer. Old Moe shuffled more lithely into the next row, and then stumbled and fell into a thorny cotton plant.

"God-damned you! You good-for-nuthin niggra! Ah'll show ya!" The overseer swore as he took three long steps toward the fallen field hand. His raised right arm was drawing the deadly bullwhip back as it snaked behind him, almost in its customary straight line. But this time, instead of rising up into its cruel arch and lashing forward towards its target, it caught on something and with a powerful jerk it pulled the overseer backwards, flying with a thump onto the ground.

The something that jerked the tail of the whip was the muscular left arm of Moses Articoke McMaster. As a stunned Horatio Doolittle looked up in surprise, the blinding sunlight glinted off an arcing hoe blade as it flew towards his face. The overseer already owned a vicious scar that curved from the bridge of his red nose, across his left cheekbone and ended somewhere past his ear; the result of a long-ago bar fight. Now the hoe of Moses sliced through the stubby neck of the overseer and severed his jugular vein.

Old Moe leapt to his feet with the agility of a young colt and threw an arm over his young conspirator's shoulder.

"Praise da Lord, Jeezus! You've done kilt him good! We's done with dat bad man fer good! Praise you, Moses! Praise you! "

"Ahhhhh... he's jus' the beginnin' Ole Moe. Now da hard part starts."

"Oh, yass!Yew betcha! Da fat's in da fire now!"

Up at the big house, Col. Rex Wilberton sat down to breakfast as usual, with his four daughters and the mistress of Wilberton Plantation.

"What day's it, Mama?" he spouted to his wife between chews of bacon and grits.

"Well, if you's a Yankee you'd know for sure, Wilber."

"It's the Fourth, ain't it Mama? Ah kin see it in the eyes of Esther an' Beulah. They go outta their way ta celebrate the Fourth. Jest ta spite us Ah'm sure! Don't matta none a'tall, Mama. OUR Independence day was the day we stood up for our rights an' kissed them damn Yankees good-bye." The four daughters giggled at their pa's usual pulling on the Northerners' noses.

July fourth was not celebrated in the C.S.A. as their Independence Day as it was in the Land of Lincoln. The Southern day of national celebration was April 14th, in honor of the firing on Fort Sumpter; the start of Dixie's road to Independence. So this July 4, 1876 meant nothing to the ruler of Wilberton Plantation in Decatur, Georgia. But to the slaves of Decatur County, who made up 74% of the total population, July 4th meant everything. It was to be their day of reckoning, the beginning of their fight for freedom.

This was the day the slaves on every plantation in the county had chosen for their long-planned revolt. This was the day that would mark the beginning of their liberation. All knew it would end in "Liberty or Death"-- as the conspiring pastors of their separate churches had discretely preached over many months of Sundays.

As Moses McMaster had muttered solemnly to Old Moe, "Now da hard part starts". And it was to start just before midnight when everyone in the plantation and the county was asleep.

Five miles down the Decatur Road, about a mile outside the town, lay the most prosperous cotton farm in the county. As mean and nasty as the overseer at Wilberton Plantation had been, the master at Sunny Creek was far worse. He had earned a reputation as the harshest slave master in the county, as experienced by the unfortunate 130 slaves who toiled in his fields.

The grandfather clock in the hall at Sunny Creek manor house had just chimed 11:45. Not a candle flickered in the great house. In the slave quarters along the creek banks no candles flickered either. But no slaves were asleep, not even the children.

Five miles back up the road at Wilberton manor, Master Rex had stayed up an hour past his usual bedtime, waiting for his overseer.

"Ah'll give that lazy good-fer-nuthin' what fer tomorrow mawnin' when tha sucker gets back home from his latest drunken binge!" Old Moe had told the master, that "yassuh, Mister Doolittle had taken to the jug soon's they's done with the day's work."

"Ah don't doubt it! That lazy bastahd's always in the bottle or the jug. Soon's you see him sneakin' back ta the barn, you tell him Ah want's ta see him. Yah hear!" The Master snorted as his face grew redder.

"Yassuh, Mastah, Ah tells him. Ah'll tell 'im soon's Ah lays eyes on 'im!" Old Moe bowed and backed out of the Manor doorway. He trembled at the thought of what tonight would bring to the master and his family. He liked the master. Master Wilberton had always been good to him and for the most part, fair to every slave who followed the strict rules. It was only the drunken overseer who took out his demons on the hides of his work force. Nevertheless, Master Wilberton should have known the broken bones and frequent cuts and "accidents" were the work of his overseer. Tonight the blindfolded Goddess of Justice would come down from above with a harsh judgment.

Five miles up the road to Decatur, the mantle clock was a few minutes ahead of the hallway grandfather clock. When it chimed midnight, 35 armed slaves watching each door to the Sunny Creek manor house looked at each other in confusion. Timing was everything the conspirators had stressed. Attack quietly just before midnight. Now they were late, even though in the grand scheme, minutes didn't matter much. But coordination did.

At Sunny Creek, a lifetime of hatred and frustration boiled over. By the time the Grandfather clock chimed fifteen minutes past midnight, every bedroom was a bloody mess. Every member of the plantation family had been hacked to death where they slept. Even the seven year old twin daughters. The house nannies tried to prevent the extremes of vengeance, but the field hands pushed them aside.

They gathered up the household's weapons; rifle, sword, pistol and ammunition and added them to their arsenal of knives, sickles, axes, hatchets and one machete. In the stables they saddled the horses and rode down the Decatur Road to their designated meeting place with the slaves from all the conspiring plantations.

"What's the meaning of this?" demanded Master Rex Wilberton, standing protectively in front of his wife.

"We're takin' our freedom, Massa Wilberton," said Moses McMaster. "Don't try ta interfere an' we won't hurt you or the missus or the chillun. We've done kilt Overseer Doolittle fer all the hurts he's done ta us over tha years. You'se been as good ta us as any kin expect, but that overseer had it cummin'. We'se gunna take us all the guns an'ammanishun you'se got, an' go join up with our Army of Liberation. We may not succeed, but we'll die tryin.'"

"You damn right you'll die tryin'! Master Wilberton raised a defiant fist round his head, puffing red-faced at Moses. "Dyin's what you'all's got comin' once the army gets a hold of yah! You must be outta yore minds ta think any good'll come of whatever yah think you're gunna do! You're all mad, I tell yah!"

"Like Ah said, Massa Wilberton. We won't hurt you or any of your family, long's ya don't try ta interfere. We're leaving 10 men here to keep things quiet, but we want the guns an' the horses."

The Master of Wilberton Plantation stared down the barrel of the shotgun in the grip of one of the field hands he knew to be dangerous. This particular slave had been disciplined many times and was possibly more embittered than any other. Rex Wilberton would have preferred to have his family's fate in the hands of Old Moe, or even this Moses McMaster. So he struggled to control his outrage and his humiliation. He clamped his mouth shut as he glared at his captors. Bide your time, Rex. Bide your time.

Horses and wagons streamed down the road to Decatur. The destination of the revolting slave army was the arsenal and the jail house. Over 250 slaves had gathered from the ten nearest plantations and were all hastening toward town. They formed a well armed mob that was about to become bigger and better armed.

Sheriff Ogilvie, his deputy and the Mayor and two clerks were up late with their mash-whiskey and branch-water poker game.

"The hell you do, Willie! Your god-damn three deuces don't ne-vah beat mah flush! You tell him, Ralphie! You knows the rules of Hoyle better'n any one!"

Before the hand was decided, the jailhouse door flew open and two shotguns blasted the late night stud disputers. Mayor, sheriff and all hands reeled out of their chairs in an explosion of blood and guts as 51 cards flew in all directions. The 52nd card, the ace of spades, slid out of the left cuff of the mayor's coat sleeve and settled into a puddle of blood trickling on the floor.

"We got 'em all, Ruffus! Grab them rifles and pistols and don't leave no ammanishun in no drawers! Let's high-tail it ovah ta tha arsenal!"

By daybreak on the morning of July 5th, a growing army of re-volting slaves numbered close to 500. They were now well stocked with rifles and ammunition. If they chose to, they could hold off the county militia and possibly the State Guards. But that was not their strategy. The plan was to gather all slaves willing to join the rebellion and as quickly as they could move men, women and children, set up fortifications on the coastal islands, where 90% of the population was African. They hoped to negotiate a stalemate and bargain for a free state with the Richmond government. They knew it was a desperate gamble.

The Liberator
July 5, 1876

Willard P. Doubleday Knox, or P.D. Knox as he was known, was neither tall nor heavy. He looked too slight and wiry to be a 50 year old field hand. But he was a survivor, and the whip scars on his back were proof of his mettle. In spite of the years of violence he had suffered, he still retained the gentle manners of his childhood. As a youngster, Willard had been treated well as the house boy in Master Knox's mansion. Willard had learned to read and write, and read most of the books in his master's library. He read Cicero's essays and Gibbon's *Rise and Fall of the Roman Empire*. And at his master's insistence, he read and reread the entire Bible. Abruptly, at age 18, Willard's world fell apart. The old master died, and his son sold Willard and many others to pay junior's gambling debts.

The new planter boss was a hard task master who hated the idea that a mere negro house boy had more book learning than he did. He told his overseer to see to it that P.D., as he called Willard, got no special treatment. In fact, the opposite. For the next 30 years, P.D. got the biting lash of the whip or the handle of the cane. But then came the long night of July 5th. Hell rode over Willard's hated plantation and vengeance filled the night with blood and screams. Willard and 120 slaves rode in the pre-dawn darkness to their rendez-vous with fate in the downtown square of Decatur, Georgia. The crowd he addressed stood silent and anxious.

"I see a time when we will be the rulers of our lives, our farms and yes, OUR COUNTRY! But first we must FIGHT for those rights. The Great Jehovah above will decide if now is the time. And as the Bible teaches, God Helps Those Who Help Themselves!" Cheers of Amen! Amen! echoed through the assemblage of 2000 black and brown faces. " I see a time when our oppressors will have no choice but to treat us as equals. The Bible tells us to go forth and multiply. And so we have. We outnumber our enemy in many of the counties of Georgia, and once we gather up all our folks from every plantation across this country, not even General Robert E. Lee's le-gions can stand against us. Now is our time! Now is our time to stand up and declare our freedom, just as the white folks stood up against first England and now recently against the Yankee folks. Now it is *your* turn to take up arms against the tyranny of those who would keep you in chains. I for one am ready to pledge my honor, my liberty and my life in our great cause for freedom." Again the assembled black and brown sea of faces roared out their Amens!

Willard Phineas Doubleday Knox quieted them with a raised hand. He continued with a solemn voice.

"Our fight will not be easy. Many of us will die. So will many of the army Richmond will send against us. They will have cannon. But so will we. We will empty every arsenal between here and the sea. We will arm ourselves and build a mighty fortress on the coastal is-lands. I cannot promise you that we will succeed, but I can promise that we will fight to the last man. As a famous Virginian said before their war with England, 'Give us Liberty! Or Give us Death!' They may kill us all, but they will pay a heavy price."

"Our numbers have grown now and in many places we are too many to be ignored any longer. Sooner or later, our oppressors must reach an understanding with us. We will no longer quietly take their whip and their chains. God knows we shall be free or die trying!"

Cheers and "Amen! Brother, Amen!" echoed across the Decatur town square.

"We have taken Decatur. We can hold the town and wait for an army to be sent against us, but we will not. We will march to the sea islands and fortify our villages there where our people outnumber the white folks ten-to-one. There we will make our stand and fight. I see that sooner or later, our enemies will find the wisdom to let us go. Like Moses told Pharaoh, 'You must let our People Go!' So must our enemies let us go!" Amen! Amen, Brother! Amen! roared the crowd.

"But make no mistake... we can never live in harmony with the white folks. There is too much bad blood. They will live in their world and we will live in ours. They will never see us as equals, and they will not give us our land without a long and bloody fight. But I see a time when *they* live on *their* land and *we* live on *ours*. They may never see us as equals, but that don't matter; we will live free and we will have *OUR OWN COUNTRY!*" The crowd erupted in an endless cheer.

A Declaration
July 10, 1876

The Secretary of the Treasury handed the letter to President Lee. "Ah cain't read this sir, let someone else read out this crap!" He threw the pages on the cabinet table.

President Robert E. Lee already knew the contents, but not everyone in his cabinet had read the letter. It was from the leader of the slave rebellion, Willard Phineas Doubleday Knox. Lee reached out and gathered up the scattered pages. He read aloud to his cabinet:

"A DECLARATION OF INDEPENDENCE --   *We hold these truths to be self evident, that ALL MEN are created EQUAL, that they are endowed by their Creator with certain unalienable rights* --- Lee smiled wryly, "They spelled IN-alienable wrong."
.... *"that among these are life, liberty and the pursuit of happiness."*

"We the free peoples of the states of Georgia, Alabama, and South Carolina, do now and forevermore declare ourselves to be free men. We declare to our oppressors that we now firmly resolve to throw off our shackles of slavery and from this day forward live on territory that we shall liberate for ourselves, our children and our children's children."

"We implore the Government of the Confederate States of America .... in the words of Moses in the time of the Pharaoh of Egypt.... LET MY PEOPLE GO! From this day forward, we pledge our lives and our sacred honor to our cause of Freedom. In the words of Patrick Henry, Give us Liberty or Give us Death!"

"Treason! Treason!" shouted Secretary of War Philip Bastionne. "They want liberty or death? Their liberty will *be* their death!"

"And then what?" answered a weary Robert E. Lee. "Do you think that'll be the end of it? I doubt it. Once that genie's out of the bottle, there will be no putting it back in. No, gentlemen, if we were looking at a few rebellious slaves it'd be a simple matter for the army or the state militia even. But this is the beginning of something bigger. I foresee that this is the prelude to a long drawn out guerrilla war that neither the colored folks or we can profit by. Either way we turn, both sides lose. I don't doubt we can put down their rebellion, but at what cost?"

The Secretary of War interrupted: "Good God, man! What are you saying? Of course we must beat them down. Our way of life is at stake. Once you let them think they can break away, bloody our noses and take a chunk of our sovereign state of Georgia, or South Carolina, then this monster will breathe more life and death. Of course we must crush the head of this snake now, before it grows more powerful!"

"I know war better than you do, Philip, with all respect. This is not an end, this is a beginning. My own slaves would sooner join this movement, even though they have always been treated kindly and fairly. But they value their freedom just as strongly as you or I do, Philip. And now they are too many for anyone to push back in the bottle. It's not their first bid for freedom; it won't be their last. Yes, we can send an army to put them down. But they are desperate men. I fought black battalions in our war against the Yankees. Give them arms and they will fight as fiercely as we did. Give them a cause for their freedom and you have a vicious battle on your hands. So we fight them and win. At what cost in our lives? And just as important, for what gain? They lose their lives; you lose the very property you're trying to hold onto. No gentlemen, I see that the genie's out of the bottle. Now we have to decide how to live with it. Think it over tonight and we'll meet tomorrow to discuss our options."

A Fateful Decision
July 11, 1876

President Lee reconvened his meeting of the cabinet. He had asked for each member's sense of the situation. Representative Oliver "Buttermilk" Stantion, Speaker of the House, jumped up out of his chair.

"Ah knew this was a-cummin' gen'lemen! Y'all recollect way back when Ah told ya's how ta boil a frog, Loo'sianna style. Well, gen'lemen, this shere frog's done jumpt outta da boilin' pot an inta da fire! An he's gunna drag us'n inta da fire with 'im! Now the question is, how does we avoid gettin' burnt?"

The Secretary of War interrupted Buttermilk with a fist on the table. "That ain't the question, Buttermilk! The issue we gotta decide is how to keep the black people in their place with the least harm to *US!* But the first problem here is how do we deal with them today. Today! Not tomorrow or next year, but right now! We got us a slave uprising on our hands. So what's the best way to restore law and order. THAT IS THE ISSUE we gotta come to grips with!"

One by one the cabinet members offered their opinions. When the last one had finished, the room went silent. All eyes turned to the president. Robert E. Lee drew a long sigh. He felt like King Solomon judging the case of the disputed baby with two mothers. He struggled under the weight of the decision. Finally he spoke.

"This is a situation that we all must have known would occur sooner or later. When my father, Henry "Light Horse" Lee was faced with this issue at the Continental Congress, he chose to pass the resolution on to a later generation. When Lincoln was elected by the Northern States, we were faced once again with the choice of how to resolve the issue. We chose to contain it within our boundaries and live with what we thought was strictly our own business. The Yankees chose otherwise and fought to settle the issue--and change our culture to better fit theirs."

"As you may or may not remember, the English Parliament voted to abolish the importation and the owning of slaves early in the century. But of course, they were not dependent on this labor force as we are. We are dependent on slave labor, some more than others. Our rural poor have never owned a single slave, nor could they afford to. Yet they joined our regiments to drive the Union armies out of our country. That was a bloody war that almost bled us dry. Too many of our finest young men died then. Too many of my best officers lie in hallowed graves as sacrifices to our way of life."

"And yet, some of you advocate for another civil war. A war that so quickly could spread like a grass fire into a protracted guerrilla war. A civil war that the Yankees would watch with smiling faces. And a reproach of "chickens coming home to roost.""

"And whose sons and grandsons would be the first to die in this civil war you clamor for? Mine, for sure. Yours, too. And when all the battlefield blood had dried what would the gain be? At best, we would quickly snuff out an insurrection. At best, only a few hundreds or thousands of lives would be lost."

"And then? Would everyone peacefully return to the old ways? Do you imagine that our slaves would just shrug and say, well, we tried, we gave it our best shot?"

"Not likely, gentlemen. Not likely. No, once again, history is calling us to *FINALLY* resolve the issue of slavery in our nation. We can take the step the English Parliament took and pass a law that ends slavery on our plantations and towns. But we all know, too many powerful folks would fight us tooth and nail. I believe Butter-milk hit on the best solution earlier. Unfortunately, that resolution did not satisfy a black population that is now numbering too many to be ignored, in too many districts. And, more to the point, they now realize this as much as we do."

"You will not like this, and many in this land will call me a trai-tor to my people and my country. But I propose that we offer a truce to this rebel mob -- army--whatever we want to call them, and sit down to discuss a peaceful resolution. As some of you may know,

President George Washington wrote into his will that upon his death, his slaves should all become freed men. And that those who chose to continue living and working his lands should become tenants and pay rents and receive wages for their labors; just as he would have agreed with any poor white farmer. Some chose this life, some chose to go north."

Secretary of War Stantion rose, red-faced and grim. "Yes! Lee. Washington freed his hands to hire out as tenants. But he did it AF-TER he was dead and buried. Are we now so dead as Washington? Do we now declare ourselves and our lifestyles dead and gone?"

"Do not think of what has been for ourselves, Phillip. Think of what lies ahead for your children's grandchildren. Think of how we can make a new order that will serve your grandchildren best. That is the opportunity facing us today. *Our* parents ignored the problem in their time; they shoved it on to us. Do we now sit back, fight another costly internal war and leave it for our children or their children to somehow solve?"

"One thing is certain, gentlemen. In my time I have witnessed the black population of Alexandria county and most of Virginia grow to the point of threatening to overwhelm us. What do you suppose happens when, God forbid, the slaves outnumber us by 10, then 20, then 30 percent? In those counties of Georgia and South Carolina where this revolt began and is now spreading, even as we sit here deciding the fate of our nation, the slaves count for up to 85 percent, yes 85 percent of the population! If you think we can forever keep this powder keg from exploding, then you miscalculate both mathematics and human nature." Lee folded his hands on the tabletop and looked wearily around at the solemn faces. No one spoke, not even the war secretary.

After what seemed a too awkward delay, the Speaker of the House rose and leaned on the edge of the cabinet table. "Ah will write up a draft resolution and try ta have it ready fer a tomorrow meetin'. But Ah would like a committee of at least two, plus you, Gen'ral Robert. And then we'll see what kind of a tempest this stirs up in the House and Senate. Y'all remember what happened last time we tried to 'boil the frog.' God help us! Again."

Marching Orders
August, 1876

President Lee sat at his large oval desk surrounded by piles of papers; reports from the various state legislatures. All were in furious rebellion against him. The were not about to grant Lee any authority to make executive decisions that went against each state's special interests. The resolution that amounted to bargaining away their wealth as the price of a peaceful negotiated settlement with a mob of empowered slaves, in revolt against their masters, and who had already committed unforgivable atrocities against innocent women and children was more than they would tolerate. Lee or no Lee, war hero or not; the old man has lost his senses, gone totally senile, no longer fit for office. That was the general reaction to Resolution #893.

Each state had only their own interests at heart. It was plain to President Lee that none shared a common vision for the good of all. He had tried valiantly for two and a half terms to lead the Confederate States by example. He rewrote his will so as to free his own slaves upon his death. His estate would then hire them as tenant farmers, ensuring a decent living for all. He made this act known to the press and suggested all slave owners should follow his example as best they could. Few were disposed to follow his generous plan.

In response to the overwhelming opposition to Lee's Slavery Resolution, the great man decided to resign the presidency. He knew his noble ambition to resolve the dilemma of slavery had failed. The larger cotton plantations had only grown in their dependency on the cheapest labor available. They could not loosen their grip on the tiger's tail. Their economics outweighed Lee's morality.

Robert E. Lee was tired. He was 69 years old. He had done all he could for his country. Other men would now wrestle with the forces that threatened to pull Old Dixie apart at the seams. It was time to step aside. He drafted his resignation letter to his countrymen.

As a war leader, Lee knew the road ahead would be wet with blood of slave and slave holder. There would be no peaceful end to it. Only when both sides had bled near death would they lay down arms and talk sensibly. He never doubted that the army and militias of the C.S.A would beat down the insurrection. And he knew once again that would only delay the inevitable, final clash. What, he wondered, would happen in counties of certain states when the ever growing black population outnumbered the whites? What would happen when the black population overwhelmed the states where whites now held absolute power? Rebellion was certain to flare up again. Guerrilla warfare? How long could the men in power keep the political and social lid on this boiling pot? He understood it was men's natural urge to be free, even slaves and ex-slaves who grew up knowing nothing but servitude.

Was his beloved Dixie inevitably marching towards its own Civil War? How ironic he thought, that the forces that drove him and others to fight off the threat of Union shackles would sooner or later cause the black people of the South to themselves fight off their own shackles. He shuddered at the thought of the enormous bloodshed that his three terms as president had not enabled him to avoid. The thunderous consequences rolled over and over in his head like a roaring headache of battlefield cannon blasts.

He had done all he could. They would not listen. They would not follow him. He had looked a long way down the road of "What's to Come" and he feared for his Old Dominion and its way of life. But he could not change the minds of those set in their ways. Now history would determine the final outcome. Now let another ambitious, younger man give the nation its marching orders. Lee had done all he could. Now, he had one last campaign to fulfill.

The Final Campaign
December, 1878

The neatly lettered gilt name on the office door at Washington & Lee University read simply "President." The old man stood behind his desk and stared out the window at the sunset beyond the oak treed ridge. A light knock on the door made him turn his head half away from the glow outside the window. The golden rays held his attention as they haloed the silver wisps curled back over his long-lobed ears.

"S'cuse me, Marse Robert," interrupted the president's steward, humbly. "But yoh said fou' thurdy, an' Ah've done brung yoh yore tea-ah, Suh."

"Thank you, Jesse. Thank you, kindly."

President Robert E. Lee took the hot cup and gazed out at the fading sunset of the winter solstice. Something about the sundown and its mood brought him back to a nagging thought had that preyed on his mind ever since that fateful event in July, 1863, fifteen years earlier. He recalled a particular lesson from his West Point days; a classroom discussion about Napoleon Bonaparte's "fan" tactic. Cadet Lee was a lifelong fan of the military genius that was Napoleon. "The Little Corsican" often split his force into separate groups and enveloped a superior enemy with several inferior numbered units. Those then converged upon the enemy like a fan being folded. The usual result was the rout of the beleaguered enemy, attacked simultaneously from several directions. It was like hounds bothering a bear.

Why recall this maneuver just now, on the shortest day of the year? Many times he'd gone over and over in his mind his own fan maneuver planned for that fateful day at Gettysburg. Many times he'd pondered what a glorious battlefield maneuver it would have been had fate allowed him to execute his plan. Many times in his mind a nagging thought had plagued him; what if the proposed Napoleonic Fan of his Grand Plan had failed to close on the Union forces as designed? After all, the Old Man knew it was military folly for an inferior force to attack a superior foe entrenched on such a formidable hilltop position as the Union Army held at Gettysburg.

Therefore, so much greater the glory in gaining an impossible victory in such a challenging situation. He imagined many times the fame attached to the name of General Robert E. Lee, Commander of the Army of Northern Virginia on that glorious and fateful day when he pulled off one of the most brilliant military maneuvers ever attempted. His old hero, Napoleon himself, would have smiled up at him in admiration. And the Grand Plan would forever be etched into the annals at West Point and discussed wherever military strategists and students studied.

But Lee had been sedated and resting in the hospital tent that fateful morning when his Grand Strategy was meant to unfold. The execution of his battle plan had been passed to his immediate subordinate, "Old Pete" Longstreet, by nature a much more cautious and conservative soldier than the Old Man. Had he been awake, Gen.

Lee would have ordered Old Pete to faithfully carry out The Plan. Lee had the utmost faith in each of the four critical elements of his fan. Old Pete would throw his entire force of 22,000 against the Union flank waiting on Little Round Top and the south end of Cemetery Ridge. General Ewell would simultaneously attack the opposite flank of Gen. Meade's' 100,000 man force dug in atop the northern end of Cemetery Ridge at Culp's Hill. At the same time Gen. Pickett would line up his 12,500 men all along the base of the wide open slope facing the center of the Union Line with its artillery concentrated along the crest of Cemetery Ridge. But the surprise tactic in the entire operation hinged on one critical element, and that was entrusted to "The Invincibles", Gen. Jeb. Stuart's 9,500 man elite cavalry unit.

The Old Man had an unflinching faith in his Invincibles. When, upon the given signal, Jeb Stuart crashed into the rear of the unprepared and unsuspecting Union Line, the cannon facing Pickett's parading men would not have time to turn and face the surprise charge of Stuart. The panic all along the Union Line would have been complete; the rout would have been stunning. The victory would have been Lee's. And yet, after all these years, the Old Man still stared out windows at brilliant sunsets and wondered: what if?

"What if the fan had stalled?" he muttered to himself.

"Wha'zat, Marse Robert? Yoh tea's gittin' cole."

The Old General turned to look sadly at Jesse, offering his tea from a shaky hand. The dying rays of the Solstice sunset framed the white wisps around the General's long-lobed ears with a last golden halo. He stepped out of the light and took his steward's offering.

"That be all, Marse Robert?" Jesse sensed an uneasiness in his boss's demeanor.

"Jesse, can Ah ask you something? You know Ah've signed the papers granting all my household hands their freedom upon my death, and providing them their livelihoods on the plantation as long as they live; same as I gave you."

"Awhhh! Marse Robert, don't say such things! You gonna outlive us all, you knows dat. You'se got lottsa days left, Suh! Lottsa days."

"No, Ah didn't mean that. Ah was gettin' to the fact that you'all would now be free to vote, if you lived in the North. You could vote for a Yankee president if you lived in Pennsylvania or New Yawk. That's what your freedom means if you lived with the Yankees. It got me thinking about the coming election up there. I've heard reports about how the Abolitionist Party has put up a Quaker to run and, yes, believe it or not, there's rumors he floated the thought about choosing a freed Negro man as his running-mate. Just for symbolic value, Ah'm sure. What are your thoughts on that, Jesse? A Negro man, as a symbol of the Abolitionist Party, running for Vice President of the North? Wouldn't that be something?"

"Oh mah Gawd, yass Suh! Thadda surely be sumpin' Marse Robert. Wou'n dat be sumpin! Why yoh may'se well be 'magining a black man as *Pres'den* while'se yo'se *'magining*. He, he, he! Yassh, a black pres'den in dah White House! Or even as da Vice Pres'den! Why, Marse Robert, dattle be dah day. Dattle be dah day when pigs learns tah fly! Yah Suh! Dattle be when pigs learns tah fly!"

Lee rubbed the inside of his left arm just above the elbow. It felt funny again, like it had several mornings for the past week. Twice this morning he had bent down to reach for papers in the bottom drawer of his desk. Both times his head spun and he felt light-headed with a buzzing in his ears. He'd quickly sat down, fearing he might faint to the floor. His doctor had pronounced him fit as ever, but he didn't feel right. Just walking up the three flights of stairs to his office had recently become a chore. He was tired by the time he reached his chair. Now here was this dizziness again. And the throbbing pulse inside his arm.

Robert E. Lee went to bed early that night. He felt very tired. About five in the morning he awoke in a sweat. A nightmare had visited him again, like it often had done since those days, fifteen years ago when on that first day of battle at Gettysburg he'd gone back to his field tent for a rest and woke up four days later. The dark dream was always the same; he was leading a charge up a long slope, through a field of ripening wheat, with shells and canisters exploding all around him. Traveller was bucking in fear when a bomb burst so near it sent clods of dirt into his face.

Then in slow motion, he was falling backward off his horse, while waving his saber over his head. Then all was black. He'd pondered it's meaning many times. He looked at the east window. The sky was still black. He sank back into his pillow and took himself back to his "Grand Plan." If only he'd been on his feet that fateful day at Gettysburg to direct his battle plan. It was as brilliant as it was bold. Napoleon would have been proud of him. The long "fish hook" position of the Union Army snaked all along the crests of Culp's Hill, Cemetery Ridge, Big Round Top and Little Round Top. As fortified as their position seemed, as well dug in as they appeared to be, he had quickly grasped the flaw in the Union position. He realized immediately that the Union flanks could not support each other. Cannon on Culp's Hill could not respond to an attack on their left flank at Round Top, and cannon on Little Round Top could not defend an attack on Culp. The weakness of the Union line was that it was too thin, too drawn out and could not be maneuvered. It was an inflexible, dug-in line. And he saw immediately that a classic "fan" maneuver of Napoleon's favorite tactic would certainly destroy either flank before the center or the furthest flank could lend its support. Meade's men would be chopped up piece-meal.

If only he had been allowed to execute his brilliant four-pronged attack as planned! What a glorious and utter victory would have been his; should have been his. In his dream state, he envisioned the victory as planned. He exhaled in a long, slow, resigned sigh.

He now saw himself in a large, dark room, a chamber whose high corners seemed far away above him. He was floating. An ethereal mist swirled slowly around him There was the booming of far off thunder; which he immediately recognized as the song of the War God. Lee felt himself floating high above the battlefield, the long Union lines spread out below. There was Slocum on the far Union right flank, dug in on Culp's Hill. The Iron Brigade of Gen. Hancock guarded the crest of Cemetery Hill and spread all the way along the spine of Cemetery Ridge. A line of cannon, ominously silent, guarded the entire ridge.

Almost below Lee's floating knees was that devil Chamberlain's Rock of Maine, lodged stubbornly in the Devil's Den. And holding fast on the extreme left flank of the Union's lines were the troops of Sickles and Sedgwick. The entire Union position looked impregnable, resolutely strong. But Lee knew it's weakness. And as he floated high above the unfolding drama, the players in his grand plan began to move, inexorably and in slow-motion.

First Jubal Early and Ewell's entire division wheeled around the end of Slocum's position on Culp's Hill and attacked the weakest point in the Union line. Early and Ewell rolled up the defenders who were in each other's line of fire. Simultaneously, Hood and Longstreet proceeded to roll up the other end of the fish hook at the Union's left flank on the Round Tops. A sudden enfilade movement stunned the defenders, Sickles and Sedgwick, while the Rock of Maine huddled uninvolved in their den.

Lee watched at the slow quadrille danced dreamily below. Now A.P. Hill moved resolutely against the embattled troops on Cemetery Hill confronting Ewell's enfilade, while Picket's 12,500 began their slow parade march in full view of the cannon of Hancock all along the strong center of the Union line waiting on the crest of Cemetery Ridge. Now came the coup de grace--a swift movement suddenly unfolding along the Baltimore Pike. It was the 9,500 horsemen of Stuart's Invincibles, galloping up the slope directly behind the Union center. As Hancock's cannon thundered a warning towards Picket's parade, Jeb Stuart raked the entire line of men in blue, creating chaos as he obliterated the Union cannoneers and rocketeers.

Faced with a simultaneous attack, before, aside and behind, Meade's men ran in panic towards their only open lane of escape. Lee had left only one small area not under attack; a narrow passage where the Baltimore Pike ran behind Cemetery Hill. The Union men who chose to retreat, formed up and slogged down the path to the Pike. The ones who chose to fight to the death holding their positions, got their wish or surrendered.

To the south, Chamberlain charged out of his den into the teeth of the victorious Alabamans and Texans of Longstreet's division who had chewed up the entire Union left flank. The continuous, mad drama danced below Lee's vision in the misty clouds that now swirled to hide the scene.

Lee half awoke from his dream. This time it did not end in a nightmare. This time the dream unfolded just as he had always planned. Lee closed his eyes and sunk deeper into his feather pillow. A contented smile crossed his thin lips. His brow was still partly damp from the earlier nightmare. A long, low sigh again escaped his relaxed mouth, followed by a deep rattle somewhere in the back of his throat. Mind and body relaxed. And he lay still.

When Jesse went to wake his master two hours later, Lee was dead; a faint hint of a satisfied smile frozen on his face. At the end of his last dream he saw himself charging along Picket's line, urging his men on, triumphantly waving his saber high above Traveller's arched neck. *The final victory was his.*

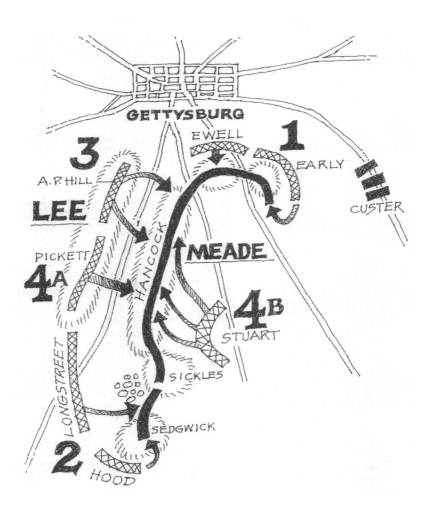

Lee's Original "Fan" Strategy
(Four Simultaneous Attacks)

Three days after the President of Washington & Lee College died, his 125 African-American slaves gained their freedom. They were free to live and work for wages at Lee's Arlington Plantation. Or, if so inclined, they were free to walk North to work for wages in Yankee factories and pay rent and buy groceries and feed their families, just like everyone else. Jesse chose to remain in Mrs. Lee's household and serve his old master's family. Others chose the promise of the North. Some chose to remain.

"Somewhere Over Yonder"
Waynesboro, Virginia
July 1, 1885

Beuford rocked gently back and forth, looking out over the fifty yards wide swath of clover field that stretched from his woods almost up to the porch. Junior would be mowing that field pretty soon he thought. Beuford's joints ached too much now to help out on the farm; that and other chores were now up to his two sons. After all, their adjoining farms were handy enough to help Beuford on the old family farm. That left Beuford and his wife Molly to sit out on the porch and enjoy summer evenings. Molly was finishing the dishes.

He lit his pipe and reached down to stroke General Ewell's head. The old blue tick hound responded with a lick of his master's hand, enjoying the saltiness offered. The July heat still lay thick up on the porch, so heavy and empty of breeze that the pipe smoke gathered around and above Beuford's head and hung there with nary a zephyr to chase it away. As he gazed over the clover field in the late twilight he noticed the first flickering of the evening's fireflies. An old war wound made him shift in his rocker and awakened a memory of twenty years earlier on a fateful day at a little village in Pennsylvania; Gettysburg. As the fireflies flitted and exploded in numbers, the entire clover field was soon lit up like the recreation of a fierce battlefield. The miniature explosions transported Beuford's mind back to a similar scene on the slopes of Culp's Hill, when his regiment tried mightily to fight its way up the hillside while hundreds of Union shells burst overhead and among the hard-charging Confederates.

The swirling dance of a field full of fireflies so convinced Beuford that he was reliving that battle scene that he instinctively ducked low in his rocker and covered his ears from the imagined shell bursts.

The hound looked up in his master's face and let out a low whimper. He sensed Beuford's sudden anguish and fear. Beuford could feel the rivulets of sweat trickle down the back of his shirt while the front became soaked with the addition of the July evening's humidity.

Beuford recalled that the entire slope of Culp's Hill had been shrouded in a sickly sulfurous cloud of gun smoke as the battle seesawed near the enemy line. He was there when the first line of Confederates was beaten back from the entrenched Union defenders on the ridge. General Ewell, the namesake of Beuford's hound, had been beaten. Ewell's orders from Lee had been to "attack the Union position and, *if practicable, continue the attack* and gain the hill from the enemy." The attack had failed, but Beuford had survived, and he still carried a shrapnel souvenir of the event.

It was not the old wound's pain that now disturbed Beuford. It was the damp sweat that covered his rail-thin body, along with a new pain that now crept under his jaw and joined the throbbing ache that pulsed up the inside of his left arm and now into his chest. The cloud of pipe smoke had grown and now gathered around his neck and head as he leaned back, gasping against the slats of his rocker. His breaths were heavy and labored and he dropped his smoldering pipe on the porch floor. Beuford tugged at the neck of his shirt in an effort to gain more breath from the mule weight that seemed to sit on his chest. General Ewell let out a plaintive whine in recognition of his master's distress. The dog laid his head on Beuford's lap, while the thin, sweat-soaked wraith in the rocker drew labored, gasping breaths.

The pipe lay still on the porch floor. The last smoldering ember in the bowl flickered as if in answer to the field of fireflies. Then it was dead. So was Beuford. General Ewell let out a low, mournful whine. He knew.

The spirit of Beuford Forrest Ralston, War Hero and Corporal of the 40th Virginia Infantry Regiment, Waynesboro Volunteers, wafted through the humid evening air among the sparkling fireflies above the field of clover. It soared over the undulating ridges of the blue gray Alleghenies until it joined rank with a long winding line of uniformed marchers, at whose head a lone figure in butternut gray, with crimson waist sash, shimmering gold epaulets and a wide brimmed campaign hat rode pine tree straight on a dappled gray *Traveller*. The spirit of Beuford Ralston stepped with the light foot of a seventeen-year-old as the long gray line crossed over into somewhere beyond yonder.

Author's Notes

With the exception of the actual historic figures in this story, all the other characters and many of the events are fictitious. The author does not intend any similarity of these fictional characters to anyone, living or dead, past or present.

Only the facts and the historic figures of the first day of the battle are based on actual events at Gettysburg. What followed are pure conjecture and fantasy as the author imagined they might have happened if Lee's supposed heart attack had caused history to take a different path.

Many of the place names in the story are also fictitious. Any alterations of actual places are meant to be taken as "artistic license" to enhance the story line and are not intended to be viewed as misrepresentations. All events after the battle are also pure fiction.

As to how this story might actually play out in the future, is left to each reader's imagination, according to their point of view on the subject. All anyone knows for certain is that this is a scenario that is still evolving; no one knows how it will eventually end.

Slavery and its aftermath is one of the major acts in the Great American Drama, that social and political experiment that began when the first indentured servants and slaves were brought here 400 years ago as cheap labor by people eager to build a better life for themselves, while escaping the social injustices of Europe.

About the Author

I am a fan of history, especially early American and European. I have always been fascinated with those twists and turns of fateful events that have altered the course of history. One such pivotal event of course, is the battle at Gettysburg.

I was intrigued by how a military genius like Robert E. Lee could have made such an apparent military miscalculation as he seemed to have done with a frontal attack, in broad daylight, in an open field, against an entrenched enemy on a hill. Was there something missing, something lost in the record? Could there have been something in Lee's plan that we never heard about?

Yes, according to that "Grey Ghost" of the Confederacy, Col. John Mosby, Lee actually had something else in mind for that fateful day in July. In his memoirs, Mosby lays out a stunning strategy for Lee that unexpectedly went awry.

In my remake of the event and its aftermath, I have given the battle an entirely different twist. I hope the reader enjoys this revision of history, and contemplates with me what might have happened if General Robert E. Lee had gained a stunning victory at Gettysburg.

M.N. Franson, July 4, 2017

The author's writing background consists of a thirty-plus year career as an advertising agency copywriter and art director, in New York City and Syracuse, NY. He lives in Syracuse with his wife and one of his two daughters, plus a Shi-Tzu named "Rowan."

ACKNOWLEDGMENTS

The author gratefully acknowledges the contributions of Col, John S. Mosby, Confederate guerrilla cavalry leader whose memoirs caused the author to revisit the Battle of Gettysburg.

Also by the author
The Wineland Sagas

An historical fiction trilogy about the
Lost Viking Colonies of North America.

Were there Vikings in America, 600 years before the Pilgrims? Yes! According to *THE WINELAND SAGAS*, Leif's relatives and descendants established settlements and trading posts among their Indian allies along the New England and Canadian Maritime coast. From the time of Leif's exploration in 1003-5, through the middle of the 16th century, a small group of determined Norsemen struggled against overwhelming odds to survive and prosper in the wilderness of North America. What happened and when and how, forms the background for the three novels of this alternate history trilogy:

I	*The Saga of Leif "the Lucky"*
II	*The Battle for Wineland*
III	*The Last Viking in Wineland*

The three sagas are available in print at Amazon.com and at Barnes & Noble.com and also in digital format at Amazon's Kindle epub books and Barnes & Noble's epub outlet, Nook Press.

Made in the USA
Columbia, SC
15 January 2018